Summer Bay

Her Yankee Heart

Written By:

Juliana Love

Unless otherwise noted: Scripture taken from the New King James Version. Copyright © 1979, 1980, 1982 by Thomas Nelson, Inc. Used by permission. All rights reserved. Unless otherwise noted, all quotations and speeches are used by Fair Use or Public Domain. Unless otherwise noted, all poems are written by the author and are copyrighted under Round Top Publishers & Productions

Copyright © 2013, 2014 Juliana Love
Summer Ray – Her Yankee Heart (Volume 3)
All rights reserved. No part of this publication may be reproduced, stored in a retrieval system, or transmitted in any form or by any means, electronic, mechanical, photocopying, recording, or otherwise, without the prior written permission of the publisher.

Front Cover photographed by J & J Photography

Round Top Publishers of Everwood Entities

Juliana Love

P.O. Box 4166 Gettysburg, PA 17325

Facebook – "Productions J3:16"

DEDICATIONS

My dedications are never without my family.

Nicole, Susan, Chris & Taylor

My four amazing children who I love

to the universe and back!

Kevin, Emily, Josh

I love you more than you know.

So very thankful to God he brought you into our lives!

I am blessed!

ACKNOWLEDGEMENTS

I would like to thank

everyone of my cast and crew of Summer Ray.

You are my extended family and

I love you all so much.

Thank you for your continued support

of our movie projects and all we are accomplishing
TOGETHER!

A SPECIAL DEDICATION AND THANK YOU!

She calls herself a "Loyal Fan of Summer Ray"

But I am honored to call her my

"Loyal Friend"

Carol, you are simply Heaven sent and

I love and appreciate you so very much!

Thank you for your excellent input.

Oh and the ghosts at our monthly girls night out thank you too! LOL

8

TABLE OF CONTENTS

INTRODUCTION....15

CHAPTER ONE

The Moment in Time....21

Unbelievable Horror....25

Circle and Cycle of Life....29

CHAPTER TWO

The Fields of Gettysburg....37

Damn Yankee....42

Summer's Dreams....48

The Real Handicap....52

CHAPTER THREE

Southern Pride...57

CHAPTER FOUR

Serenity Hope....63

CHAPTER FIVE

Finally....67

Tangled Mess....72

New State of Mind....76

Father Time....82

New Found Focus....85

CHAPTER SIX

The Light....91

One of Us....95

Destiny....102

CHAPTER SEVEN

The Séance....107

CHAPTER EIGHT

Her Own Union Legacy....117

Sixty Seven Minutes....121

CHAPTER NINE

Reality....135

Own Little World....140

CHAPTER TEN

Battle Scars....155

CHAPTER ELEVEN

Past and Present....135

CHAPTER TWELVE

Her Handkerchief....169

A Rude Awakening....174

The Spirit of the South....182

CHAPTER THIRTEEN

A Sign….189

The Journey of a Million Miles….193

Acts of Terrorism….199

The Sunken Road….204

The Battle of Antietam….213

Monocacy Battlefield….216

CHAPTER FOURTEEN

The Hard Rock Café….223

CHAPTER FIFTEEN

Newly Reunited….231

The Past Thirty Years…232

Her Sacrifice….234

OTHER BOOKS BY THE AUTHOR

245

A NOTE FROM THE AUTHOR

247

INTRODUCTION

So far, this volume is my favorite. I love the new characters and the new settings, past and present. This volume, though the shortest in the series, is definitely the turning point.

So many unanswered questions such as: Does Summer Ray make it in time? Will she chose the right one to stand by? Who does her heart's desire really turn out to be? Will they find Anthony? What does Charleston, South Carolina have to do with the story now? Who are Corine and the Matron Laurise? Why does Anastasia or present day Summer Ray, an abolitionist, own slaves?

As the clock is ticking and for a selected few, time is running out. Some of these questions must be answered as the characters are now racing against time. If you have followed along with our journey of Summer Ray, you surely know by now that the "Summer Ray – Series" is not just another Civil War story, but it truly is an epic adventure. "The Journey Home?" Well, we are almost there, but first things indeed still need to be first.

THE YOU IN ME

I stood by you, for a second here,
And it felt like eternity.
To have you close, to feel you near,
Meant the world to me.

Speechless was I, as I looked into,
Such passionate and beautiful eyes.
It was almost as if, I could see right through,
Each and every disguise.

You smiled at me, I smiled back,
I have not let go.
What was missing before, what I did lack,
Now at least I know.

For a split second in time, I had it all!
Now there's just an empty space.
With both our backs against a wall,
Circumstance, it took your place.

So, I will stay quiet and rest awhile,
No one will know that I am here.
Though a picture can paint your amazing smile,
It can't feel or hold you near.

Sleepless nights, mind wandering far,
A hint of sadness I'm not with you.
Yet it doesn't matter where you are,
I am there a time, times two.

But I will stay quiet, not make a sound,
And somehow just let you be.
Hoping soon, you'll come back around,
Looking for the you in me!

"We hold these truths to be self evident that all men are created equal, endowed by their Creator with certain unalienable rights, that among these are life, liberty and the pursuit of happiness."

Declaration of Independence

July 4, 1776

CHAPTER ONE

The Moment in Time

Summer, rocking steadily back and forth on her white wicker rocking chair was staring intently out into the open air of her new backyard in Gettysburg. Finally taking the plunge to cross the Pennsylvania state line, she left her Maryland roots just south of the Mason Dixon line. Her own backyard, complete with a few boulders, streams and tall trees, Summer often spent the night out on her deck, in hopes she would encounter familiar ghost spirits or perhaps meet new ones.

Yet ever since the departure of the General McDaniels, the disappointing and dreadful eerie silence, as always, spoke loud and clear of the emptiness surrounding both her environment as well as inside her own heart. Though it was early morning and Summer was sipping her vanilla creamed coffee, though the birds were chirping, cows mooing in neighboring fields and helicopters flying overhead, all she could hear was the lack of resonance from the soldiers she knew that were supposed to be there.

Nevertheless, faithful to the core of a true American Soldier, the Unknowns and the Union Lt. Colonel George Jameson did not leave Savannah, Georgia. The Union and Confederate General of the US Unknown Soldiers, Michael Moses McDaniels was left in the torment of Madeline's bonds, along with the Confederate Colonel JD Marsh. The mystery of the pocket watch Summer held in her possession, still had to be solved.

Yet time needed to heal Summer Ray's broken heart. She could not begin the process of seeking the necessary clues for such an answer as to why Madeline gave the watch to the Confederate Colonel JD Marsh in the first place, until she was fully recovered of the bruises the General so savagely inflicted upon her. Summer's maternal grandmother, the Shaman, knew but simply could not express it to her grand-daughter. In fact, after Summer Ray was able to climb out of her shell of dis-enchantment, though still unable to confront the fire witch or return to Georgia she introduced her grandmother to the Gatekeeper and low and behold they married. Both of them at the tender age of 92 years old, like it was meant to be all along.

Happy endings are never out of reach, even if they may take years to produce. What does it matter when love can touch a human at any given moment in time and make up for all the lost years? The moment in time when everything instantly changes and you are no longer the same as you were the second before love unexpectedly appeared. When the same sun, moon and stars, suddenly look brighter and the universe flows with more meaning. The oceans, birds and even the trees come to life in a greater measure as they roar and sing to the beating of your newfound flash of inspiration and motivation. You sit and wonder at how all at once, your heart, soul and mind can think of nothing else. Like a wave of the sea, love washes over you and that one person in all the world, touches your life like no one else ever could. To know this kind of existence is one of the greatest gifts of God.

Seeing Summer's grandmother as happy as the circumstances allowed her, gave Summer a sense of hope that her own true love would eventually find her. But first things indeed had to be first. Now that Summer's grandmother was finally reunited with her and her great grandson Billy, with a great-great grand-daughter on the way, what was so savagely stolen from the Shaman in the early years was certainly being brought back. Though Summer's real mother Natasha wasn't present in human form, somehow she lingered on with them in spirit. Yet, Anthony was another mystery to be solved as to who he was and his whereabouts. Summer knew she had to find him to free the men in chains and to begin a new life with her beloved twin as well.

Be that as it may, as she was quietly rocking back and forth, her mind was on something else. Something etched in the shadows of her mind. Unspeakable words she could not express to most humans, especially Yankee ones.

God forbid that something, unfortunately, turned out to be true!

Unbelievable Horror

While staring off into space, it was more of President Abraham Lincoln that Summer was recollecting. The South, in the Civil War era with the tremendous beauty and glamour of ball gowns, antebellum homes and Southern gentleman, still produced in some cities, an evil such that has tainted the blighted landscape ever since. Men, women and children, owned like cattle. Masters who whipped the very flesh off their backs should a negro become insubordinate, defiant or rebellious. How about just plain exhausted from working out in the cotton fields day after day, with the barest necessities to keep them alive.

To top it off, when Summer Ray found out that just a few miles from her childhood home, once stood the 2nd largest slave working plantation in Maryland, right along the Monocacy River, she could hardly stand it. A diehard Yankee woman to the core, all the history drilled into her while growing up, how could so much be omitted? Summer learned that in 1793, a French family by the name of the Vinvendieres came to Frederick County, Maryland from Saint-Domingue which in present day is Haiti. The family brought with them twelve slaves. By the early 1800's the Vinvendieres, against the law of the land at the time, exceeded the maximum amount of slaves allowed from twelve to a disgusting brood of ninety!

    Even owning one slave, was one too many. The brutal and cruel treatment of these slaves was documented by a man named, Julian Niemcewicz, a Polish aristocrat. On June 15, 1798 he recorded the following:

"Four miles from the town, Frederick we forded the river Monocacy.

On its banks one can see a row of wooden houses and one stone house with the upper storeys painted white. This is the residence of a Frenchman called Payant (Jean Payen de Bosisneuf; a distant relatives of the Vinvendieres', who left Saint-Domingue with a substantial sum and with it bought a few hundred negroes whom he treats with the greatest tyranny. One can see on the home farm instruments of torture, stocks, wooden horses, whips, etc. Two or three negroes have crippled with torture have brought legal action against him, but the matter has not yet been settled.

This man is 60 years old, without children or relatives; he keeps an old French woman Magnan Vinvendiere with two daughters; she in sweetness of humor, even surpasses him. This charming group has caused about 50 legal actions to be brought. They foam with rage, beat the negroes, complain and fight with each other. In these ways does this man use his wealth, and comforts his life in its decent toward the grave."

Such unbelievable horror to behold in both the North and the South, even well into the 21st Century that "America the Beautiful" could have ever condoned the ugliness of slavery. Rep. Steve Cohen (D-TN) on July 29, 2008 stated the following:

"The fact is slavery and Jim Crow are stains upon what is the greatest nation on the face of the earth."

An "Official Apology for Slavery" was given by Congress, six months after the first African-American was elected to President. But as Senator Tom Harkin stated:

> "Slavery, Jim Crow laws, and their lasting consequences, however, are an enduring national shame."

Summer was torn. Her Yankee heart had been abruptly challenged. Yet, back in her Gettysburg home, away from the South, she was able to at the very least begin to heal from the General's abrupt dismissal of her. Though not one of his soldiers to command and yet somehow Summer was treated as such. Her removal from the General's life was irrevocably and crystal clear. For many months after, words escaped her. Her relocation to Gettysburg, though productive, was just another way for her to be closer to him though she was far from admitting it.

Circle and Cycle of Life

One of the luxuries of Summer Ray's backyard was the fact the nearest neighbor was a half a mile away. Her privacy mattered to her. Fervent in her love for animals, she even started a home refugee for abandoned cats and dogs. Her animals and the ones she cared for until adoption simply made her happy. Though, like her close friends the Pickett's, adoption day always brought with it happy and sad tears. Every time Summer brought home a new rescue, she swore she wouldn't get attached. But those closest to her knew better. Still, her son Billy and his new wife Emma gave Summer Ray the sense that the circle and cycle of life, both were of great importance. Life has a way of renewing itself, if one can just be patient.

    Summer's backyard backed up to what else, Big Round Top. The sound of the morning birds, with insects chirping and the sunrays beaming through the trees, Summer had harmony with the nature surrounding her. But, she was greatly lacking peace with in her own soul. Her work was far from finished. She knew it was just a matter of time before she would have to venture out with Kat to find the answers to all the unanswered questions. The pocket watch, of the Confederate Colonel Joseph David Marsh was a symbol of time past, present and future.

To renew something meant that something before it was either dead or outdated. Time is much too valuable to waste. It is much too precious and is a privilege to contain. Yet so many people refuse to take care of it as if it were the beating of their own heart. Which in reality, it is. Once a human's heart stops beating, time for them on planet earth also stops. So how can one take such a precious commodity as time and throw it away, as if it were nothing more than a worthless piece of rubbish? Summer, having come to close to having time taken from her, learned the art of gratitude for every breath she was still allowed to breathe, even if that meant some of those breaths were still in pain.

Still not fully recovered from her accident in her early years, the pain was getting harder and harder for Summer to grapple with. The over 50 mark was starting to take its toll on her stiff muscle and joints. Only if her pain was unbearable would she take her doctor prescribed narcotic pain medication. It was only by the grace of God she could move at all without it. Summer couldn't slow time down, but she also couldn't speed it up either. There was always this need for one or the other, yet she could never accomplish the impossible. Time was held only in God's hands. Summer had to wait on Him, whether she liked it or not.

Summer's cell phone rang and she answered, "Hey." Kat's voice was on the other end, "So are you still sitting there staring out into space?"

Summer replied, "Nope not anymore. I am looking at the open air of nothingness. I have been trying to read 'Uncle Tom's Cabin.' But have made it only to chapter three. Distracted I guess."

Kat laughed and said, "Well at least that is progress. So what are we doing tonight? Do you want to go to the Avenue for dinner, your favorite waitress Brooke might be working or we could go to Dunlaps?"

Summer inquired, "Uh how about you come here and we invite the kids for some meatloaf and mashed potatoes."

Kat reminded Summer, "You know, you are the only one of us who actually still likes that meal. But, since it would make you happy and maybe cheer you up, sure. I will get in touch with Ella and Ellodie and you call Billy and Emma. See you around 3?"

Summer replied, "Sure that sounds good. Love you bye." As Summer tried to hang up her cell, she heard Kat say, "Summer Ray?"

A quizzical Summer answered, "Yes Kat. What is it?"

Her best friend answered, "We will find him, Anthony that is."

Summer agreed and said, "We will Kat. I just don't know where to begin. See you soon okay?"

Kat said her goodbyes and Summer quietly whispered, "Goodbye." Hanging up her cell and putting it back on her lap, Summer began to pray. God knew where her twin brother was and she believed at just the right time, He would reveal just where. As Summer looked at her watch, it was now only 11:15 in the morning. Out in the cool autumn breeze with the temperature in the low 70's, she laid the book on her lap and slowly rocked herself to sleep.

I Am Born Again

Remove the cobwebs from off my mind,
So that I can remember you.
Never again to leave you behind,
I want you with me it's true.

Though I don't know how or where to begin,
To become what I should be.
Still with you, I know, I am born again,
Though I know, we don't always agree.

You must understand, I stand my ground,
My beliefs are who I am.
Yet in you, perfectly, love does abound,
I want only to hold your hand.

And walk with you no matter where,
I am lost without your smile.
My beloved and friend for you I'm there,
No matter the struggle nor mile.

So remove the cobwebs from off my mind,
So it is truly you that I can see.
And in your arms please let me find,
The most perfect part of me.

CHAPTER TWO

The Fields of Gettysburg

Charleston, South Carolina, 1867

"Miss Anastasia?" A young Negro slave asked as she frantically woke her up. The Mistress Anastasia was on the front porch of her southern home, or what was left of it after the Yankees came through and ransacked and stole almost everything her and her husband ever owned. Luckily, whether it was a blessing or a curse, Anastasia was never quite sure. At least those damn Yanks left her house still standing. Unbeknown to Anastasia, God answered the prayer of her beloved husband. As he lay dying on the fields of Gettysburg, clutching the handkerchief she sewed for him, with his dying breath he whispered, "God, please do not let them take Serenity and please look after my Annie." Then he joined the other thousands of men who never opened their eyes again this side of Heaven in human form, due to that horrid war.

After rocking herself to sleep, in the midst of peaceful dreams, the rude yet soft awakening by her servant Hannah, almost abruptly Anastasia answered,

"Yes Hannah! What is it?"

Her servant answered, "Pardon me ma-am, but there seems to be a gentleman come a calling for ya. He is in the parlor and boy is he a handsome ma-am." Anastasia stood to her feet and brushed the wrinkles out of her ragged day dress. As she looked in the mirror, she adjusted her bodice with the girl's help and carefully aligned her long black curls. Standing tall, just like a Confederate Battle Flag that had survived the war all tattered and stained with smoke, Anastasia asked, "Who is it? Did he say?"

Hannah answered, "No ma-am. He just sayz it's impotant. I needs to brush your hair ma-am. You can'ts seez no gentleman, a Yankee General lookin all unladylike, now cans ya?"

In the war torn south quite a few of Anastasia's slaves enlisted and some were forced to fight in the Union and Confederate Armies. Out of the fourteen male slaves, nine of them came back to Anastasia in South Carolina. Three of her slaves with their families settled north of the Mason Dixon line in Harrisburg, PA. Though they struggled having to attend to their new life, Anastasia was happy they were content. They often wrote her letters and promised to visit. Yet, somewhere in Anastasia's mind, she knew they were gone for good. She knew if she had asked, out of their loyalty to her and her husband, they would have come back. But, Anastasia refused to stand in the way of their freedom.

Elijah, who enlisted with the Confederate Army, while fighting in Georgia, came face to face with his beloved friend Cooper. They grew up together on the plantation. The boys as youngsters would often run up to Anastasia, beaming with pride as they learned to read a new word. Cooper, who wore the Blue, both men were ordered to shoot and neither one could. The bonds that held them, was greater than any side they fought for. Sadly, they were deemed "Traitors to the Cause" and Elijah was hung and Cooper was sent to Andersonville Prison where he died of dysentery. When word reached Anastasia of their brutal deaths, she mourned for months. Black or white, she loved them as if they were part of her own soul.

Gabriel, Frederick, Joseph, Francis, Phillip, Solomon, William, Vincent, and Peter, miraculously survived the war and though offered their freedom, returned home to the only home they knew. Unfortunately, the home they used to be acquainted with was barely recognizable. Yet, upon hearing the sad news of how their "Massa" was killed at Gettysburg, upon their return, they vowed to stay with Miss Anastasia, work the land and raise their families once again at Serenity. With her husband gone, the plantation was more than what Anastasia could bear on her own. The

South, though sympathetic, was still unable to assist her as it too had crumbled under the heavy lashing of General William Tecumseh Sherman during his "March to the Sea," as well as a four year long bombardment from the Union.

Anastasia's beautiful home with black shutters on every window, a white veranda encasing the brick house with beautiful white pillars, a light blue door all surrounded by gardens was sadly neglected. Though not a mansion like other plantation homes, it was home none the less to Anastasia. Most of the horses that the family also raised were stolen by Yankee rebels. Anastasia's nails, hands and face, were hardened from the long hours working the fields. Yet, the hardship of war had matured her features and were even more striking as she wasn't so weak and delicate looking. She was only thirty-two years old and widowed. But she knew she was not the only widow and in a morbid sort of way, it gave her a sense that she wasn't alone in her suffering. Luckily, the time of her "Widow's Weeds" attire had passed. She no longer had to work the fields in astonishingly hot black clothes. Yet, the summer sun and the harsh reality of starting over, the cruelty of an ageless time sparked a new fervor in her. She and Serenity survived and for that she knew there was a purpose.

Damn Yankee

As she approached the parlor, the smell of cherry tobacco permeated the hallway. Fearing it was another damn Yankee wanting to rape her or set her house on fire, she grabbed the nearest musket she could find. Turning the corner to the parlor, she held the rifle up to her shoulder and cocked it ever so slightly. Yet, she wasn't prepared for the sight of such a man as this. He on the other hand was not prepared at the courage of this bedraggled woman. The Union General cautiously approached her and said, "There is no need for the rifle ma-am. I mean you no harm."

Anastasia demanded, "Who are you and what do you want."

The General replied, "I want to help you. You see, your husband, Captain Armistead Adams, during Pickett's Charge ma-am, well he refused to shoot me though I only stood a foot away from him. He saluted me instead and that act of patriotism cost him his life." Anastasia put the rifle down by her side and said, "My husband was a good man General. He loved his God, his country and his family. But, there is no need. We are managing."

The General looked around at his impoverished surroundings and stated, "Pardon me Ma-am, but from the looks of things, 'The Restoration of the South' could take several years." Anastasia turned to Hannah and asked, "Could you please bring out some tea for the good General here." The now shy servant sadly whispered, "But ma-am, don't ya remember, we are outs of tea and haz been for dayz now."

Anastasia asked, "Coffee, anything?" Hannah languished, "No ma-am. We ain't got a nuthin in the cuppards."

The General stated, "Ms. Adams, your husband saved my life. It has taken me years to find you. I would be simply returning a debt if you allowed me to help you in return."

Anastasia pointed to the General's uniform and asked, "Well General Sir, are you prepared to help in such a way that it will get your hands dirty? Your uniform seems to be without wear and tear."

An almost insulted General replied, "I am prepared to repay a debt and to pay my respects to the wife of a very brave and gallant officer of the Confederate Army."

Anastasia angrily replied, "Yes, but the rest of the Yankee army was not as considerate. They came through here and pillaged almost everything we ever owned."

The General asked, "Including your slaves?" Anastasia, now on the verge of tears, angrily replied, "Our slaves General were and still are our family."

The General asked, "How could something you own be your family? Dogs, cats and horses some consider family. But they are not human. Slaves are men, women and children."

Hannah and another slave Solomon, who spoke the clearest English of all the slaves, came to their mistress's rescue as they stood by Anastasia and Solomon spoke, "Ms. Adams, Sir, never mistreats us. She gives us shelter, food, education and a home. The others left because they wuz afraid."

The General asked, "Afraid of what, freedom?"

Solomon replied, "No Sir! Afraid youz Yanks weren't who you sazs you wuz. Because the North won the war, they wuz afraid Mr. Lincoln wouldn't keep hiz word seeing that he didn't see us Negro's as equal when he waz elected. Seeing how the war waz not started on account of us negroes as most Northern white folk like to claim it waz. But we in the South know different. The North also had slaves that no one liked to talk about before the war started here in Charleston. Slavery waz nothin more than an excuse to invade our land Sir."

The handsome Union General was taken a back at the blinding truth of what Solomon had said. Still not wanting to agree or disagree, he only spoke, "North or South, slavery has been an evil since the conception of the United States began in the 1600's."

Anastasia interrupted, "If you would like to help General, there is cotton that needs to be picked. So if you will excuse me that is where I will be." An angry Anastasia pulled up her tattered day dress by the broken hoop skirt underneath it and defiantly pushed her way passed the General outside to the fields. The small twenty five acres she and her husband owned before the Civil War, only fourteen of those acres could be salvaged for crops and five acres were plotted for her slaves and their families. The remaining six acres were left in ashes. The "Boys in Blue" burnt and torched them along with the barn when they stole the family horses. All of the loss combined, instilled upon Anastasia her own version of the "Rebel Yell." She was grief stricken on so many different levels.

The hot Southern sun beat down on her, as she pulled her straw hat down further on her head. Much to her surprise, the General took off his frock and vest and pulled up his sleeves to his white cotton shirt, as he too began to pick cotton.

When Anastasia looked up at him she spoke, "I am sure this isn't what you had in mind, now is it General. I know I should hate you, but that would mar my good husband's memory."

Summer's Dreams

She wailed as a thorn pricked deep into her finger, "Ouch." Time stopped.

Summer back in Gettysburg, woke up and clutching her right hand she softly whispered, "What the?" She looked at her watch and it was only 11:45am. "I have only been asleep for a few minutes?" she sighed. "This cool breeze is really starting to get to me," she thought. The book she was reading "Uncle Tom's Cabin" had fallen off her lap onto the deck floor. She picked it up and then placed it on the table beside her rocking chair. Her beloved Sammy, a Border Collie was still by her feet curled up on his blue dog bed snoring away as if he hadn't had a care in the world. The other two dogs were enjoying the autumn breeze on the grass near the stream. They never wander far. The property surrounding her home had a buried electric fence. The two cats, Betsy a calico and Bennett a tabby, lounged around on the top railings of the deck.

Summer's dreams were starting to freak her out. She sat there and pondered what was real and what was fake. Two time periods seem to have overlapped at her expense and she could never quite understand the reasoning behind it. So the fake wasn't really false, but rather misplaced. It was almost as if the two centuries were also locked in mortal combat, but why? Why could the era of the Civil War not find its rest? Why was the past still so present in the future? What did Summer Ray Sherwood have to do with history and dear God when would she be free of it? Or was it her lot in life to carry the burdens of the ageless battlefields to help those spirits she could to cross over?

As a Christian she struggled with her beliefs. Christianity had almost lost its flavor to her and she refused to be just another hypocrite. Her God was everything to her, but her beliefs about Gay and Lesbian marriage, birth control and other political stands, caused many of her Christian brothers and sisters to question the authenticity of her relationship to the Father. Still

Summer didn't budge. If God had a problem with her, He was quite able to tell her so. Though she read and studied the Bible, and she knew it was God's Word, she also knew that she did not have a right to impose her own religious beliefs on anyone. You cannot live with peace with your neighbor if you force your will on them, can you? Just because Summer was against a same sex marriage in her own life, she did not have the right to judge or demand that of another human life. In doing so, slavery would once again be alive and well on planet Earth.

Though Summer's life was anything less than normal, she knew she was blessed. Perhaps it was her own near death experience that opened the portal to the Unknowns. "That would explain a lot, "Summer thought then asked herself, "But what about Kat? She didn't almost die?" Sitting back on her rocking chair, slowly rocking back and forth once again, Summer silently ached for the only life she had asked God for, a loving husband to share her family with. Yet somehow with all of life's twists and turns, like the stream rolling before her, to get somewhere you have to follow the path God forged and not stray from it as eventually that path will lead to purpose and answered prayer.

Sam became a blur to Summer Ray as she simply gave up hope of a happy life with him. The General could never be Summer's husband as he lived over a 100 years before she was even born. As Summer pondered, the memories of things lost began to fill her heart with great sadness. Things appeared so hopeless to her and she just did not envision her futuristic life to be that "can't eat and can't sleep" kind of future with her newly found soul mate. Summer just needed to turn yet another page in the chapter of her life, as what was waiting for her on the other side of that page was a love so perfect it would feel as if it were too good to be true.

Yet she had to cut herself off from all of the traps she enslaved herself with. Self doubt is one of the greatest enemies of the gifts of God. She had to learn to believe that it could really happen.

Her dreams really could come true. But with so much disappointment and trauma from her past, she feared the honesty of a new life. She ran from the presence of love as if it were the devil himself. Summer had to finally cross over from the death of her old self to the acceptance of her new self as she was now and not pretend she was someone she could never be again. She was whole as an injured woman from a very severe car accident. Her fears followed her through the years and she still has not yet recovered. She fills her time doing, when perhaps she needs to sit still and simply accept. Her self denial never matured her gracefully. Her athleticism kept her fit but her spirit is still searching for the real her to finally awaken.

The Real Handicap

Summer has yet to admit that her disabilities are not damaging to her as a woman or a mother. Her disabilities in her eyes, keeps men away from her. When in reality, it is this warped sense of self that is the real handicap. Her thoughts of, "If I could just learn to cook, or talk right, or go back to college; If I could just stay young and forever thin" haunt Ms. Summer Ray Sherwood like a black snake wrapped around her neck trying to choke the life out of her.

Who she was Summer really did not know. Her ice skating was imbedded into her soul. Her music from her childhood had long since been gone. But she swore someday she would find the time to relearn the guitar and piano. She promised herself she would sing again and not be afraid to stand in front of a crowd on stage and sing the songs she had written. Yet, if you look in her cherry Hope Chest, there those songs lay. They are full of dust with no hope of ever finding the right tune as her three guitars and her mother's baby grand piano are also left neglected and unattended as well. Summer's greatest fear since her accident is failure. She is always so scared someone will laugh at her and make fun of her. Her foolish pride must be shattered if she ever hope to become the woman God created her to be. Someday...!

Yet someday never comes as there is always something more important on Summer Ray's plate. Or perhaps it is her constant fear that she is not good enough, at least not since her accident some thirty years before. When competing as a Figure Skater she felt like a million bucks, even if she lost. The ice made her feel like someone. It gave her wings that she could fly with and ever since that night of horror when that other car slammed head on into hers, her wings were broken and they have never been repaired. It is almost as if Summer Ray has only been existing. While at the same time, she is wandering around like the walking dead. Perhaps that is why she can connect with the General McDaniels and the others who are also the walking dead.

Yet time keeps ticking forward and Summer still cannot slow time down. As she looks in the mirror she sees that she is silently aging.

She knows the truth of what Ben Franklin once stated:

"Lost time can never be found again."

Is that why she dreams of an age gone by, to try and find the time again she lost, or thinks she has lost? Or is she really on a mission from God to bring peace to spirits she unintentionally stumbled upon? She would have to wait until their journey home to become a reality to find out. Until then she would have to still search out the clues as they are given to her. But for now, her recompense was the comfort of her rocking chair and for now she would just close her eyes once again and go if anywhere, back to the time in history that just doesn't want to die or ever be... forgotten!

CHAPTER THREE

Southern Pride

The mysterious General rushed to her side and grabbed Anastasia's now injured and bloodied hand. He then took his cotton shirt and ripped a piece of it off to wrap her hand with. Shocked at the sight of such calloused and bruised hands he asked, "What are you trying to prove. Is this just your stupid Southern pride or do you really think that you can save SERENITY on your own?"

Anastasia screamed, "Let go of me. I cannot save anything on my own General. But, I will not give up SERENITY to anyone, let alone a damn Yankee General."

The General threw her hand down and replied, "I do not want SERENITY ma-am. But the Reconstruction of the South will take time. How will you survive until then? Your Southern charm certainly is not going to carry you through." What used to be well manicured nails, gowns that were exquisite, halls filled with treasures of art, lawns landscaped with the finest of decorations and flourishing Paris had to offer, as Spanish trees adorned the short dirt driveway, were now all brutally replaced with the sorrows of the war torn South. Anastasia, knowing how shabby and worn out she looked and how unladylike she smelled from the sweat that dripped from her brow, she turned and ran from the General in tears. She knew he was right. But was not about to allow him the satisfaction of being told so.

The General ran after her and grabbed her left arm to stop her and said, "I am sorry. Anastasia, look at me." The General pulled up her straw hat so he could clearly see her tear stained face and was stunned by what he saw. The color of her eyes, a deep golden brown filled with such sadness his own heart began to ache. Underneath the sweat and grime, her demeanor took his breath away. As he assessed her face, his eyes dropped lower to the three buttons on Anastasia's day dress that were missing. As she took a deep breath, not intentionally she exposed her tender flesh. What caught his eyes and pulsated his own flesh, were the scratches across her chest that were put there mercilessly from hard labor. Her Southern pride was almost too much for him to bear. Oh how he wanted to kiss those wretched wounds of hers and carry her off into the sunset, never to be harmed again. Oh how he wanted to protect this pitiful yet defiantly strong woman he instantly came to love and disdain at the same time. He knew he could not save her lost husband. But oh how he wanted to save her, if only that meant to save her from herself.

Forgetting he was a damn Yankee, for a split second, Anastasia was in awe at how handsome he was. She knew she could get forever lost in those crystal sea blue eyes of his. Oh how she too just wanted to be wrapped in those strong arms protected, loved and cared for. Oh how she wanted to just be a lady once again; a woman of breeding and deportment, with a husband who was proud to call her his own. As she buried her face in his chest, the memories of the happier years before the war flooded her soul as she tried to contain her emotions.

The General seeing her so frail, softly lifted her chin and said, "You cannot keep SERENITY on your own. The North or South will find a way to take it from you. The trees they will come in and cut down to make new houses, is that what you want?"

Anastasia, as if reality had just hastily showed back up, pulled away from the General and shouted "You are nothing but a damn Yank and you Sir are just like those who destroyed what I am trying so hard to keep alive." An angry General shouted, "You will die Anastasia! You, your slaves… is all this damn Southern Pride worth it? Tell me is it worth it!!!"

Anastasia cut him off and bewailed, "Family, they are my family. They are the ONLY family I have left. And if I die trying, well General, at least I tried." Anastasia then said, "Good day sir. Get off my property or the next time I see you on it, I won't be as gallant as my late husband. I will shoot to kill."

Anastasia ran off toward the porch and as she went inside the house, she slammed the door behind her. As the General walked to his horse, he noticed something had fallen from Anastasia's day dress. He bent down and picked it up. He then held it close to his face, a tattered crocheted handkerchief with the words, "Anastasia Isabella Adams" sewn into it. Her husband carried this very handkerchief with him into battle. Oftentimes he would pull it out and hold it to his face, much like the General was doing. The sweet honeysuckle and rose perfume never lost its divine smell.

When Anastasia's husband was killed, a young Union private, found the handkerchief near the Peach Orchard. He then turned it over to his superior officer. The Union Army graciously sent it back to Anastasia. Shortly thereafter, word was sent by the Army of Northern Virginia, that her husband was killed at Gettysburg. He is buried in the Richmond National Cemetery, along with many of his comrades. Anastasia kept the handkerchief close to her heart, as that is where her husband kept it as well. Somehow it brought him closer and kept his memory alive.

Leaning on the other side of the slammed front door, when Anastasia reached into her bodice to retrieve the handkerchief to wipe her face, she gasped. It wasn't there! The Union General tucked it safely inside his frock and slowly trotted off toward nowhere.

CHAPTER FOUR

Serenity Hope

Summer was startled awake by the sound of a horn blowing. It was her beloved son Billy and his beautiful wife Emma, now seven months pregnant. Trying to shake herself awake from the vivid and very real dream, she softly whispered, "SERENITY." Billy helped his wife out of the car and walked over to where his momma was now standing. He hugged her and said laughing, "Wow! Did you forget you invited us over mom?"

Summer replied, "Never could I forget, just fell asleep that's all. It is very peaceful here. It isn't like Emmitsburg son, with the sounds of cars, trucks and sirens and fights on Main Street. Not to mention those stupid frat parties with the drunken college kids throwing up and tossing their beer cans in our yard. This," Summer stopped to pause and look around, then continued, "is serenity." A bewildered Summer stopped short and looked down as if to comprehend what was taking place.

Emma stepped in and asked, "Mom? Are you alright?"

Summer Ray smiled and answered, "Yes sweetie. I just have to wake up that's all. I am still a little groggy from all this fresh mountain air."

Billy told his mom as he handed her a grocery bag, "We brought ribs and steaks to cook on the grill."

Summer took the bag and firmly noted, "You son are cooking on the grill. I guess my meatloaf idea got vetoed!"

Billy laughed and said, "Ya think?"

Emma asked, "Where are the girls and Aunt Katie?"

Summer looked out toward the long drive up to her house and said, "They will be here soon. Kat can't wait to see you three."

Emma laughed, "Us three. Wow a little girl. We are still thinking of a name."

Billy answered, "Didn't you just say, 'Serenity' mom? That is very pretty. What do you think Em?"

Emma smiled and agreed, "Serenity Sherwood is perfect." Summer Ray instantly flashback to "The Blessings of Liberty," a book she encountered and read earlier in the year and often wondered by a particular devotion stuck with her. 'In these times of uncertainly...,' Summer thought, "*Jesus Christ is the same today, yesterday and forever.*" Only He is unchanging. Though 'these are the times that try men's souls,' like Thomas Paine wrote, we cannot be "summer soldiers or sunshine patriots." Yet without hope, hope of the 'times' overcoming the obstacles of evil, those hearts needed to stand and conquer, will give up as so many have already. It's a very sad state of affairs when a human soul loses hope to the point of taking their own life to end their pain of a hopeless existence.

Summer shrugged off the vision with an addition to Serenity's new name. She leaned forward closer to her daughter in law and put her hand on her unborn grand-daughter and declared, "Serenity Hope Sherwood." Billy hugged his wife and then kissed his momma on the forehead and said, "I love you mom." Summer Ray replied, "I know son. I know! And it isn't because of my famous cooking either."

CHAPTER FIVE

Finally

As laughter filled the air at the new Sherwood homestead, Summer was desperately trying to put the new pieces together. She knew the dream she just woke up from was no ordinary dream. Inwardly, Summer was grieving over the fact, in her dream, she was a slave owner. She lived at "Serenity" somewhere in Charleston, South Carolina. The thought that reincarnation was real, pierced through her mind like a bolt of lightning and immediately dismissed. But, something was lurking and Summer instinctively knew it. Like just before it rains, there is this feeling that something is coming. But, Summer didn't know if what was coming was that of a tornado or refreshing rain. Summer also knew once the BBQ was over, she would run to her office and search the internet to find out who this

General was just like she did with the Colonel McDaniels.

In the dream she was married and her husband was killed in Gettysburg, somewhere on this sacred and hallowed land she now calls home. She was Mrs. Anastasia Adams. The only Adams Summer Ray had any historical knowledge of were John and Abigail of the Revolutionary War. Was her husband a direct descendant of those Adams? At this point, nothing surprised Summer Ray. All the questions just meant more research and that was something she craved.

The Confederate Colonel JD Marsh's pocket watch was safely hidden in her jewelry box. The General Michael Moses McDaniels always took priority in Summer's thoughts. So much so, she visited his gravesite daily. It did not matter the weather. She was there, faithfully every day hoping that somehow her presence here would spark something of her presence in Georgia. Without communication, having not seen or spoken to him in over a year, Summer still believed in miracles. She knew she wasn't going to just up and leave the Confederate Colonel Marsh and the General locked up in Madeline's chains. It was just a matter of time before she herself sprung into action.

Still the immediate tugging on Summer was the fact she owned slaves in her dream and it was tormenting her. In present time, so much was messed up with the world. This is due to the rampant violence, drugs, racism and even some Christians crossing the lines of decency. When one accepted Jesus Christ as their personal Lord and Savior, upon becoming "born again," it was Summer's conviction that all races, creeds and colors were now one and that all those things did not matter. How did racism once again rear its ugly head? After all Martin Luther King Jr. fought and died for - unity and equality. There are those who pull the race card, regardless of color or creed, if they think justice was not served to their satisfaction, in some cases causing even more violent behavior. It becomes a vicious cycle.

The increasing anger toward mankind is sickening. Summer was sadly aware of the times. But if judgment begins with the household of God, she was also aware that many a Christians were in a world of trouble if they didn't stop the racism against their fellow man. She cringed with holy fear. If the church was supposed to be a Light in a very dark world; if the church is to be salt of the earth; if the light goes out and if the salt loses its flavor, where is the hope of the world getting any better? Who will God blame first? How messed up is too messed up?

Is there any hope at all of a happy life filled with life? Or has the times become so detrimental that it would be best if God just sent Jesus back like yesterday? If there is no hope, there is no future. Yet, Summer knew God would hold off as long as He could. If He could save just one more soul, He would do so. He knows how permanent Hell is once a soul is sent there. There is no escaping it. To spend eternity with Satan, there are no words on planet earth that could accurately define how utterly and undeniably horrifying that would be. George Washington once stated:

"War is Hell."

Imagine living the Civil War over and over again for all eternity. The gruesome agony of limbs blown off, men shot in the face, soldiers falling to their deaths onto boulders smashing the very bones that used to give them movement. Blood soaked, putrid smell of death everywhere, forever in pain, forever burning, to be tortured by demons and laughed at by the devil. No! There still had to be some kind of message to bring to the lost of the world before they suffered such a fate. It only made Summer Ray even more anxious to find her twin brother.

The Tangled Mess

Still pondering her dream, oh how it bothered her so. She knew she would never own slaves, not in the present or in any age of the past. It just wasn't in her being to do so. She believed wholeheartedly that "all men were created equal." Summer also wondered if Martin Luther King Jr. could come back for a day and see that state of affairs in America. What would he do? You know, like what would Jesus do? Summer grieved over the past, the present and she was desperately trying to find some hope and laughter for the future. Yet it was back to matters at hand.

The thought hit her, "Wait a minute, didn't Anthony also die here in Gettysburg? But he called himself Major Bryce Alexander Benjamin." Was this mysterious husband of hers in the Civil War, a link to her twin brother? As Billy, Emma and Summer Ray were preparing the meat for the grill, Katie, Ella and Elodie arrived. As everyone said their, 'Hello's' and exchanged hugs, Summer Ray told the others she needed to talk to her best friend. But before Summer whisked her away, Billy stepped in and said to his Aunt Katie, "Mom named the baby, Serenity Hope Sherwood."

Wow! There is something about giving names that makes things seem so real. Aunt Katie and the girls hugged Billy and Emma and Summer Ray went outside to the deck. When Kat also came outside, Summer began to tell her about the dream she had just before Billy and Emma arrived.

Kat asked, "So what do you think it means? Maybe you were just off in la la land dreaming about "Uncle Tom's Cabin."

Summer rejected her friend's conclusion and asked, "Who dreams of Uncle Tom's Cabin?" Then shaking her head she informed Kat, "No! It wasn't that. I saw him as if he were standing right here in front of me like you are. I saw all of them." A concerned Kat inquired, "Do you want to go to the cemetery and see if we can find this new General's grave?"

Summer answered, "Damnit! We can't. He didn't tell me his name. I need to call my grandmother." Kat was starting to finally see some spark of hope that somehow the tangled mess would work itself out. At times it was like watching a real life horror movie, or reading a dramatic war and romance novel. Kat knew Summer's convictions ran deep. There was no stopping Summer from fulfilling her promise to those soldiers. Although, unbeknown to her best friend, Kat silently wished she had never agreed to drive to the Tops that cold and wintery day so many many years before. Seeing her best friend so driven by this daunting force, Kat knew that a normal life, the one they dreamed about as kids, was quite possibly nothing more than a childhood fantasy. But she rested in the fact that there was still hope that someday, those dreams of theirs would all come true.

Summer dug into her back pocket and retrieved her cell phone to call the Shaman.

She answered, "Hello dear? Is everything alright?"

Summer replied, "I am not sure. We are having a cook out. Can you and the Gatekeeper please come, like now?"

Her grandmother said, "Of course dear. When will you be here to pick us up?"

Summer answered, "In about fifteen minutes, is that okay?"

The Shaman told her grand-daughter that she and the Gatekeeper would be waiting.

Summer turned to Kat and said, "I need to go and get them. Maybe this is our first clue in finding Anthony."

Kat replied, "Yes! Maybe you are finally ready."

Summer hugged her friend and said, "I hope so Katie."

"Katie? Wow! You haven't called me that in years." Kat replied. Summer used to call her Katie until her accident. For the first few years after she couldn't say Katie. So she had to shorten it to Kat and Kat was called that ever since. It was nice for her to hear her old nickname. It gave her a sense that her old "Ray, Ray" was in the verge of being resurrected.

As Billy and the girls came outside, Summer shouted up to him, "I have to go get your grandma and the Gatekeeper. Can you please start the grill son?"

Billy answered, "Yep, on my way to it now."

New State of Mind

Summer drove the back roads to get to Baltimore Street. The Gatekeeper and Shaman live across the street from East Cemetery Hill and a few doors down from the Orphanage. Summer never could drive by the Orphanage without remembering those abused orphans. Her hatred for Rosa Carmichael was just as fervent, though Rosa's spirit no longer remained in Gettysburg. Summer's only consolation was that Rosa was suffering now the same kind of torment she inflicted on those children.

Reminiscing still about her present dream, Anastasia lived in the South and she owned of all things....slaves. The thought made her cringe. As a Yankee woman, she was always 100% against slavery in present time that is. The war was over and the dream was during the Reconstruction of the South. Who the General was, she had yet to find out. There were still so many unanswered questions. Yet she missed her own beloved General McDaniels terribly.

Lost in thought, suddenly she jerked the car over by the Evergreen Cemetery and parked the car on Baltimore Street down the hill from the Gate House. She then walked up the grassy hill toward the grave of Jennie Wade. She smiled at a few tourists in the cemetery, trying to look like she was just one of them. It did not matter the thousands of times she had walked the grounds of the Evergreen and The Gettysburg National Cemetery, she never felt out of place.

Jennie Wade walked the Evergreen Cemetery and somehow that always gave Summer Ray a link to the history there. At Jennie Wade's grave is where the she physically saw the General McDaniels for the first time. His white shoulder length hair, deep dark brown eyes, a smile that caused time to stand still, his stature of over 6 feet tall; his beauty was permanently branded into Summer Ray's heart. Thinking she was just another tourist to joke around with, when Summer looked for Jack Skellys grave, the General stood behind it and pointed down. His amusement was always to see the humans fright as he instantly disappeared into thin air.

Looking to the right of Jennie Wade's grave, stands an iron fence separating the Evergreen Cemetery from the Gettysburg National Cemetery. The National Cemetery is where she cast out Rosa. All at once, Summer could see the witch rising above the treetops, orphaned children beaten, starving, dirty, bruised and crying were floating underneath her. Her wand glowed with the same green neon poison Summer saw her with before she cast her out.

Summer than ran out of the Evergreen Cemetery, through the Gate House and into the Gettysburg National Cemetery. Running and almost knocking down her grandmother and the Gatekeeper, Summer had to make sure it was just a vision and not the real spirit of the wicked Rosa Carmichael. When Summer looked up at the treetops, there was nothing. The Gatekeeper and her grandmother slowly walked up behind her and her grandmother asked, "What is it dear?"

A baffled Summer replied, "I just saw Rosa and the children they were just floating in mid air."

The Gatekeeper asked, "What do you suppose it means Summer Ray?"

After a brief pause, she answered, "Poison, it means poison." Both the Gatekeeper and her grandmother stood motionless, hoping the pieces of the puzzle would reveal themselves to Summer Ray.

Summer exclaimed as if the Light had finally broken through even Hell itself, "A spell... she cast a spell on the pocket watch. Oh My God, that's it!"

An excited Summer turned to the Gatekeeper and asked, "That's it, isn't it. Madeline cursed the pocket watch to make the Colonel Marsh fall in love with her and the General..." Summer started crying and said, "That is why he rejected me. He thought I only loved him because of the watch."

The Shaman, pleased Summer was finally given the answer, hugged her grand-daughter and said, "Yes my dear. It is the reason he rejected you. You see, it wasn't because he didn't love you. He thought you did not love him."

Summer shouted, "I have to go to him."

The five foot two Shaman quietly demanded, "Not until we find our Anthony. I will not lose you again Anastasia. How many times do I have to keep telling you that?"

The Gatekeeper replied, "Summer Ray, we must respect the dead while we are still living. Come child! This cemetery is no place for aggression. They have seen enough of that already."

Summer remembering she was on sacred ground offered her apologies for speaking so loud. Then as the three of them were walking out of the Gettysburg National Cemetery, Summer turned to the Shaman and informed her, "I have no clues grandmother. But, I had a dream right before Billy and Emma came over."

As Summer Ray proceeded to tell her grandmother and the Gatekeeper her dream, for the first time in months, Summer Ray felt "Serenity Hope" was not only her grand-daughter's new name, but also a real place in time as well as a new state of mind.

Father Time

Back at the Pennsylvania Memorial on Hancock Avenue, watching over the town of Gettysburg, Captain Talhelm informed the Angels under his command the good news. Yet he also gave a stern warning when he spoke, "We must prepare for battle in Savannah. We will be called to help Captain Xavier and the Angels guarding the Bonaventure Cemetery. Once the pieces are in place, Summer will return to Georgia. The SPIRIT has informed me Madeline is already gathering hostiles against Summer Ray and all who stand with her."

The mighty Sostar replied, "We will fight to free those souls under her spell and we will prevail."

All the Angels in earshot of what Sostar declared shouted out in unison, "Praise Be to God!"

Captain Talhelm agreed and said, "Yes my friend, we will fight. But I do not know yet the fate of the General McDaniels. Human time is still not something we can contain. His fate rests in the hands of time, Father Time and He has chosen to hide the outcome."

Rory spoke, "His will is perfect! If only Summer Ray can learn to trust in it."

Sostar asked, "What will happen to her faith, if the General doesn't make it out of Bonaventure the way he went in?"

Captain Talhelm sadly answered, "I know not the answers to the matters of the heart my brothers. We will have to wait and see. Summer feels their peace rests upon her shoulders and if she cannot obtain that peace for them, which was never hers to give, we can only hope she does not fall back."

Rory, Summer's Guardian Angel spoke loud and clear, "We must help her to stand, even it is means once again we are wounded."

Captain Talhelm commissioned the remaining Warrior Angels, "Go! Stir up the hearts of the people to pray in the SPIRIT. Though they know not what they pray for, unless they pray with the understanding. Their intercession will be a great move of God. I will go seek out the counsel of the Arch Angel Michael. If Summer leaves for Georgia before my return, go at once!"

The Angels raised their arms and voices to Heaven and exclaimed, "We will and to God be the glory!" Instantly Captain Talhelm expanded his great wings 20, 30, 40 feet in diameter and flew off disappearing into the cloud cover above the historical town of Gettysburg.

Rory and Sostar thanked God for His goodness. Summer Ray was well on her way to the final destination, of paradise for the fallen soldiers, though in reality their destination was always granted. Yet due to the loyalty of the soldiers to their General, paradise would have to wait until he too would join them.

New Found Focus

Summer had to finally come to grips with the fact, it was not a promise she could ever keep. Heaven or Hell was not in her power to grant. Her promise (though unknowing to her at the time) was only to bring peace to a bitter man of unforgiveness – The General Michael Moses McDaniels. His peace would allow the clouds of Heaven to open up for those who served under him. Even the Gatekeeper anxiously awaited their ascension into Heaven. The place where they would no longer suffer, shed a tear or hurt in anyway shape or form. They would finally brush off the residue of the brutal war they died in. Summer smiled as she thought of her beloved General and said, "Wow, no more pain. He wouldn't suffer anymore grandmother. I have to find Anthony and I have to free those men."

The Shaman held her grand-daughter's hand and answered, "I know my dear, I know."

The drive back to Summer's house, with the words "No more pain" ringing in Summer's ear, she finally understood her mission. It wasn't just to keep a soul out of Hell, but rather it was to enjoy the comfort of living pain free and without the suffering both planet Earth and Hell provided. Heaven offered the joy of seeing the Creator of the Universe and the Lord Jesus Christ, Savior of all mankind. In Heaven the streets are made of gold and more beautiful than the human heart can even comprehend. But, the most beautiful part of all, there is no sadness in Heaven. There is only love, Light and laughter. There are no more tears, no more lack, no more sickness or disease, or murder or abuse. There are no more wars, or bloodshed. Angels are without number worshipping the God of Heaven for His goodness.

Serenity and hope will surely be found in such a place as this.

Yes, Summer Ray knew the tides were rising and it was time to ride. With a new found focus of Heaven, knowing if God was for her, who could be against her, her sights were once again on Savannah, Georgia. The Bonaventure Cemetery awaited her. But, knowing it was imperative she find her twin, she turned to the Shaman and asked, "How do I find him?"

The Shaman answered, "My dear, if I knew, I would most certainly tell you." Summer than asked the Gatekeeper the same question. His reply was slow, yet stern, "The answer is hidden my child. You must search it out."

Upon arriving back at Summer's house, Kat noticed her countenance was brighter and asked, "You are glowing, why?"

Summer smiled and said, "I figured out the pocket watch Kat. I saw Rosa, the poison and the wand. Remember how she used to cast spells on the children of Gettysburg?"

Kat answered, "Yes."

Summer told her, "I did the math like the Gatekeeper told me to. Madeline put a spell on the pocket watch to make the Colonel Marsh fall in love with her. But, I still do not know why he gave it to me."

Kat said, 'The General, he must think you only loved him due to that spell."

Overhearing the bizarre conversation, Billy holding a grilling utensil in his hand asked, "What the hell are you two talking about? What pocket watch and what Colonel? Did you mention a General too?"

The Shaman walked up to her great grandson and said, "Here give your old great grandma a big hug."

As Billy hugged his great grandmother, he looked at his mom.

Summer said, "What? Son you wouldn't believe me if I told you."

Billy told him mom, "Try me."

The Shaman told Summer Ray, "It is time. He needs to know if he doesn't already."

So the family BBQ, ended up being more that what Summer Ray had bargained for. It took about an hour for her to explain the whole story to Billy, Emma, Ella and Ellodie. But, once she was finally finished, Billy spoke up and said, "Well it's about damn time. Mom don't you think I didn't notice things? You are no good at lying."

Billy asked, "So what about Uncle Anthony?"

Kat answered, "Your mother refuses to find him through witchcraft or Tarot Cards. She will not seek the dark to find the light."

Emma said, "Well that's a relief. Wow what a family I have married into. I cannot wait for our Serenity Hope Sherwood to meet you all!"

CHAPTER SIX

The Light

About a week after the family cookout, for some odd reason, Summer Ray was compelled to drive to Devil's Den. It was an early morning wakeup call around 6:00AM in late October. The following month in November, the town once again would be alive and busy with tourists for the Remembrance Day activities; the parade down Baltimore Street, the luminaries at the Gettysburg National Cemetery, President Abraham Lincoln who is usually James Getty, reciting The Gettysburg Address and the Remembrance Day Ball. So, anytime Summer could spend quiet time alone on the battlefields, she was always ever so thankful.

The weather this morning was chilly around 50 degrees, yet the sky was a brilliant blue and bursting with colors of yellow, purple and pink. Fog and mist had blanketed the base of the

Tops near Plum Run next to Devil's Den. The fall leaves had finally changed to beautiful vivid colors of red, orange and yellow. Of course she had to whip out her camera to snap off a few shots. There is such indescribable beauty, in the midst of such devastating circumstances.

On July 2, 1863, Union and Confederate Soldiers, 1,000's of them, spewed about in the rocks and boulders of Devil's Den and the slopes of Little Round Top. Plum Run saturated with their blood, and bloated bodies that floated downstream. Other soldiers baked in the hot summer sun. The Slaughter Pen it would come to be called. It was said that one could not walk the land without walking over or on top of a dead soldier. Their blood contaminated the Gettysburg water supply for years to come. Quite a few of the farmers vacated and sold off their property, as the gruesome remains of some of the dead Union and Confederate soldiers rotted the farm land. What a task of cleaning up the aftermath, the fateful town was left with. Some of the Confederates were buried in mass graves that some believe are still there. While the Yankee soldiers were eventually interred at the Soldier's Cemetery, now named the Gettysburg National Cemetery.

Summer often wondered if the spirits of these dead soldiers knew how savagely they were left behind. So many people have their own stories to tell about the Gettysburg Ghosts. Some are real. While others are nothing but money hungry liars! It angered Summer that some people would exploit the lingering spirits for their own ill gotten gain. She wondered if those idiots even knew the spirits at all. Summer knew them and loved them. She protected them and dared not expose them to a bunch of deceiving ghost people.

If the news of the General and the Unknowns ever reached the wrong hands, Summer shuddered at the thought. The quiet town of Gettysburg would be invaded by every ghost person this side of the Mason Dixon and then some. Camera crews by the millions would try to take part of the phenomenon. Summer never really took to mind the incredible miracle of it all. The General was her soul, while Sam remained her heart.

The tragic part is when some of those ghost tours companies tangle with a demon passing off as a soldier spirit. They usually run from it, instead of casting it out. Summer never had much patience for the so called mediums and psychics of Gettysburg. Although she was grateful for a few of their friendships, Summer is well known as an advocate for the Cross of Jesus Christ. She is avidly and passionately against witchcraft, white or black!

Though respectful of others beliefs, a few of her friends are also atheists. Such non belief of such a magnificent God, Summer will never understand. Her prayers reach out to them in hopes they will someday see the Light and believe in the God that she knows is real. With no sights on eternity and the hereafter, having nothing to really look forward to, life must seem so empty at times or like it goes by at sonic speed, here today and gone tomorrow. No! Summer was thankful her God is very much alive and is very much a Father. Without Him she knows she is as hopelessly lost as those atheists.

One of Us

Driving around the bottom of the Den, Summer felt nothing. So, she drove up and around the loop on top where the Witness Tree stood majestically tall. Finally, she felt some sort of conviction, pulled over and parked the car. After grabbing her camera and locking the car door, though no other humans were nearby, she then walked down toward the "Confederate Sharpshooters Nest" just below and adjacent to the Witness Tree. Having never actually gone inside the nest before, Summer decided it was time. Surrounded by stone walls and boulders, she was almost swallowed. A twinge of fear began to envelope her as she all the sudden was consciously aware of her quarters. The car accident of yesteryear left her incredibly claustrophobic. Summer was pinned in the car for over thirty minutes, as the firemen worked frantically with the "Jaws of Life" to pry her free. What seems irrational behavior at times is nothing more than what some doctors refer to as Post Traumatic Stress Disorder. As if suffering from Traumatic Brain Injury wasn't enough. The PTSD only adds insult to injury!

Summer's heart started to beat erratically as panic, once again, began to overtake her. Slowly she managed to creep up the stone wall to look up and over at Little Round Top. Luckily, her thoughts turned toward that of the Colonel Joshua Chamberlain of the 20th Maine. His gallant efforts to secure the end of the Union line made him quite the hero. The 20th Maine Monument is erected on the backside slope of Little Round Top. On October 3, 1888, the Colonel Chamberlain who was promoted to Major General, at the dedication of the 20th Maine he stated:

"Today we stand on an awful arena, where character which was the growth of centuries was tested and determined by the issues of a single day.

We are compassed about by a cloud of witnesses; not alone the shadowy ranks of those who wrestled here, but the greater parties of the action. They for whom these things were done. Forms of thought rise before us, as in an amphitheatre, circle beyond circle, rank above rank;

The State, The Union, The People. And these are One. Let us from the arena, contemplate them, the spiritual spectators."

As the sun just started to poke through the treetops and onto the wall where she stood behind, Summer snapped off a few pictures. Yet the second she reached out to touch the stone wall on her right to reposition herself, she was instantly overcome with a grief; a grief so heart wrenching, she began to cry uncontrollably. Something or someone had jumped inside her soul reminding her of the agony the soldiers suffered. Summer fell down on rocky and dirt floor inside the nest, clutched her stomach with one hand, and held the camera in the other. Alone in the hopelessness she felt, as no other humans were in the area. Summer engrossed in the moment, through her tears she cried out,

"I don't know who you are, but I am so dreadfully sorry for all you had to suffer." Slipping silently into a trance like state, an unfamiliar voice in the background spoke,

"Remember us, as though you were one of us. Our blood mixed with yours. Cherish not only the beauty of your surroundings, but cherish and remember us as well."

Summer Ray shook herself free of the strange cloak of darkness and asked, "How have I forgotten you? You are my life's work."

The voice continued, "The Unknowns are our brothers. Confederate or Union, we all were killed the same way. We died as enemies, but as you know, we were buried as brothers. We know who we are and they (though Unknown) know who they are as well. You have forgotten the blood of the named. Yet, our shed blood for the Cause was just as important. Many named are still a waiting to cross over. The grief you feel, is but a touch of the horror we carry.

Look to the fact your ancestor fought in this war. The castle on Little Round Top that you love so much, Summer Ray, is not just a fantasy full of little girl's dreams like Cinderella. The castle is a monument dedicated to the brave soldiers of the 44th and 12th New York. Yet brave soldiers on both sides of the North and South gave the ultimate sacrifice.

We cherish the work you do. We smile when you smile. We are sad when you are sad. We know you will succeed at helping to free the General and Colonel. Yet when they and the

Unknowns return to Gettysburg, will you remember us as well? Many of us are in need. Many of us are confused as time has progressed too fast for us to keep up. Look at your clothes and how you dress improper for a lady of breeding. We marvel at what we see as time for us has stopped. Yet it continues to too beat on as if progress is a good thing. Chivalry did not die when we died, yet where are the chivalrous?

Union or Confederate, we fought for a rightful Cause. Where are the manners of the 19th Century? Where is the kindness and where are the children who used to work alongside their parents? What has happened to the American home where families sat down and ate dinner together and read from the Good Book? We hear the cry of the children who are aborted as they pass through this dimension to be received by the Light. Our suffering never ceases for the condition of mankind in its current state. Ghost hunters call for us and some cause us even more unrest."

Summer through her tears questioned, "What am I supposed to do? I am not God."

The voice spoke, "No! You are not Him. We just want to be remembered, the way the Unknowns are. We want peace and serenity, the way the Unknowns do. Your promise to bring peace to them, was it meant for all of us?"

Summer anxiously replied, "Yes! Yes of course it did. I am sorry. I didn't know you needed the same resolve."

As a cold chill suddenly formed around her and as the leaves of the trees began to sway back and forth, a fire had branded and burned into her soul. Summer's newfound journey had ignited a long lost spark of revival that she was in desperate need of. The plan to save the General and the Colonel would somehow save all of them.

Destiny

As an author, turned photographer, Summer Ray, witnessed some of the most beautiful and mesmerizing sunrises and sunsets in the town of Gettysburg. Her trauma of having to leave the General McDaniels in Savannah, suddenly developed into a whole new level of providence. Her world kept expanding and she was getting smaller. Knowing this, she needed to enlist the help of others. The million dollar question, "Was the help from the living or the dead?"

Later that evening, Summer sat with her grandmother up at Little Round Top. As the Shaman pointed at the sunset,

Summer exclaimed, "I have seen that sun go down thousands of times. I will never get tired of looking at it. It's beauty is undeniable and definitely beyond description. I call it, God's Gettysburg."

The Shaman responded, "What is troubling you my dear? You are distant this evening. Is it the General?"

Summer changing the subject asked, "Do you think they knew Anthony as the Major Bryce Alexander Benjamin?"

The Shaman smiled and her only response was, "Perhaps."

Summer shook her head and said, "You know more but you are not going to tell me are you?"

The Shaman answered, "No! My dear I am not. You must follow the path God has chosen, and walk on it at His pace. If you are given the whole puzzle, you will miss the pieces along the way that are necessary to your own restoration."

Summer gave her grandmother one of those, "What the hell are you talking about" looks, but didn't dare to say it. Yet, as if reading her mind, her grandmother continued,

"Anastasia, when you were critically injured from that car accident, were you healed instantly, or was it in steps?"

Summer answered, "It was and still is a very long slow process. But, there were some things that God healed me from."

The Shaman asked, "And why do you supposed God did not heal you from your injuries right away?"

Summer leaned back against the wall and said, "I don't know grand-mother. I have asked God that question numerous times and He never answered."

The Shaman settled the matter, "If you could go back in time, like you travel to the Civil War, would you have taken a different route, so as to not have been hit by that car?"

Summer answered, "If it meant, I wouldn't be where I am today, than no. I would not."

Her grandmother stated, "Case closed. Now, stop looking back over your shoulder to what could have been and start seeing and reaching toward what can be."

Summer hugged her grandmother and said, "I am so glad I almost knocked you down in Savannah."

The Shaman answered, "It was destiny my dear, God's. Besides, He knew your old grandma wasn't about to leave planet Earth without Him keeping His promise of me finding you and Anthony. He answered my prayers to find you, and He is working on answering them to find Anthony."

Summer noticed a strange look on her grandmother's face and inquired, "What is it? You suddenly put your head down. I know something is wrong."

The Shaman simply responded, "It is not time for me to tell you."

Summer put her right arm around her grandmother and rested her head of her shoulder. As the two gazed upon another Gettysburg sunset, Summer knew she couldn't push the issue. So for now, she would just let it go. Another day was leaving, which meant a new one would be dawning. Summer whispered, "I love you grandmother."

CHAPTER SEVEN

The Séance

It was midnight at the Jennie Wade House on Baltimore Street in Gettysburg. Woeburn and his minions as usual, were out wandering the town seeking whom they may devour as ordered by their master Satan. Ghost tours were in full force at the Orphanage, the Farnsworth House, Sach's Covered Bridge and a few others in an around the battlefields. Though the park closed at 10:00pm, it really never stopped a few daring independent ghost people from breaking the rules, if it meant they would see an apparition on the battlefield.

Yet, one cannot simply will to see a phantom soldier spirit. They appear at their own time, their own way and if they have the energy to do so. Many ghosts are seen in broad daylight and are overlooked due to the more eccentric ghost tours after dark. Yet, the vast majority of ghost sightings in and around Gettysburg are not real. Orbs were nothing more than dust on the camera lens or floating around the atmosphere. Perhaps a rain drop or the sun reflection, one must be very careful not to get suckered into the deception that lurks around every corner in Gettysburg. Yet for recreational purposes, a ghost tour is a rather fun way to pass the time, if it is not taken too seriously.

As billions of stars were twinkling overhead, up at East Cemetery Hill, near the lifelike statue of the General Winfield Scott Hancock on his horse, a faint sound of a woman crying could be heard. Legend has it her Union husband was killed on that very hill. At midnight, especially when the mist blankets the ground, she, along with her shovel floats in and out of the fog, as she desperately searches for her long lost lover. Orphaned boys, the ones that Rosa Carmichael tortured, are seen following behind this despairing spirit of a widowed woman. Dressed in her black widows weeds attire, and the orphaned boys longing for a mother's love, perhaps there is some comfort to their downtrodden souls, by following after this poor grieving lady. They call her, "Lucy" and know not what for.

Safely tucked away in her own bed, was Summer Ray. If she knew what the Shaman and Kat were up to, all hell would break loose. The two ladies snuck into the basement of the Jennie Wade House, to have a séance' with the waiting Medium named Margaret. Summer, adamant and downright obstinate in her beliefs to not consult psychics or mediums, would surely be furious with her grandmother and best friend if she was to find out the truth of their antics.

The basement where a fake Jennie Wade's body lay, covered in a quilt blanket, rocking chair, this was the same basement Summer Ray had a meltdown in years before. The medium quietly instructed the Shaman and Kat to sit on the chairs, while she chanted a few prayers and lit a circle of candles around the small table. The fake arm of Jennie Wade, extended from underneath the quilt, looked so deathly real. It's ashen color, still form of a body outlined under the blanket, sent shivers down Kat's spine. Jennie Wade was one of Summer Ray's favorite romance stories. Kat knew Summer was still longing for her Jack. Her favorite movie, "Walk the Line" the story of June Carter and Johnny Cash. Nothing in the world could separate Summer Ray Sherwood from her forever bond of hopeful romantic dreams.

After the ladies all sat down on the hard non-cushioned metal chairs, Margaret turned to the Shaman and asked, "What is it that you want to know?"

The Shaman replied, 'I want to find my grandson Anthony." The medium dressed all in black, had a white and red scarf tied around her forehead. She was a young woman around thirty, petite and like Jeswood was gifted in the arts of black magic. Yet, neither the Shaman nor Kat would dare to ask Jeswood for her help. They both knew Jeswood's loyalty to Summer Ray would cause her to expose the truth. So they turned to a woman Summer knew nothing about.

As the dark, damp and dreary basement was lit by the candles, it set off an eerie glow as their shadows bounced off the basement walls. As Margaret looked intently into her crystal ball, smoke began to rise up from the floorboards. Kat, the Shaman and the medium all held hands and quietly chanted. Suddenly, Kat's face appeared on the crystal ball and Kat screamed.

The Medium turned to Kat and said, "You know her Anthony." Kat explained they had met when she travelled back in time to the Civil War."

Margaret admonished, "No, you have met him in our time period, keep chanting." A stunned Kat and Shaman did as instructed as more scenes flashed through the crystal ball when one scene in particular hit Kat like a ton of bricks.

"Oh my God," she wailed. "It's him. He's that guy that stood next to me in New York City. When Summer found out she was adopted, her dad sent her to the Rockefeller Center to ice skate. This man came and stood beside me and I remember how peaceful I felt next to him, a perfect stranger! Here she was grieving over the loss of her birthright and her real one was standing only a few feet away from her!"

The Medium turned to hopeful Shaman and informed her, "This is your Anthony."

The Shaman with tears in her eyes spoke, "He is in New York City. I knew he was alive. Thank you dear Jesus."

Kat stepped in, "Great, just great. There are 20 million people in that city. Do you know how close to impossible it will be to find him?"

Margaret stopped them both and shouted, "Wait! I see him standing in flames."

The Shaman gasped, 'Standing in flames? Is he dead?"

The Medium answered, "No! He is putting water on the fire."

Kat asked, "Is he a fireman?"

The Medium replied, "It appears so."

The Shaman responded, "Now it all makes sense. Madeline is a fire witch and why we so desperately need Anthony to release those men."

Kat interjected, "None of this makes sense. He cannot put out Madeline's flames with water."

Margaret smiled and told the Shaman, "I have to agree."

The twins grandmother stated the not so obvious, "Yes, but he can put them out with faith. Do you remember what the Bible says, *'The shield of faith can extinguish all the fiery darts of the evil one?'* Anthony is not afraid of the fire. He will not be concentrating on if he will get burnt or not, like his twin sister. Summer Ray struggles with her faith."

Kat replied, "But hasn't that been with good reason?" The Shaman answered, "We must go. The longer we stay the greater chance of her finding out what we have done."

Margaret stood up to turn the lights on, not noticing demon scouts on the basement steps. When the lights turned on, they scattered like roaches and flew off to Devil's Den to report to Woeburn.

Kat asked, "Why does it all the sudden smell like rotten eggs in here?" The Shaman knew and kept quiet.

Margaret the Medium only stated, "It is a damp cellar Kat. A lot of weird smells get trapped down here." After she bent down to blow out the candles, the Shaman had at the very least a sense of direction and Kat was not far behind her. Yet, the Shaman also knew Satan would try to stop them from ever reaching Anthony in time. In time for what? The Shaman was not permitted to say. Her darling grand-daughter would try to take on the fire witch alone. She would fail miserably in her attempts and so much would be lost to the

Underworld. No, as long a she could, the Shaman would keep the secret to herself.

CHAPTER EIGHT

Her Own Union Legacy

"Lo the winter has past, the time for the singing birds has come."

Song of Solomon

It was a Saturday spring night in April and a restless Summer Ray couldn't sleep. Tossing and turning in her queen size sleigh bed, she cussed several times at her insomnia. The time was 11:02pm and a strong thunderstorm had unexpectedly, rolled heartlessly into the small town of Gettysburg. Afraid of the surround sound the rumbling noises, most of Summer Ray's animals were at her bedside. Yet, thunderstorms, freshly laundered bed sheets and a few fluffy pillows usually, like a sweet lullaby, rocked Summer Ray gently off to sleep. Of course tonight, when she was exhausted and in desperate need a good night of restful and soothing sleep, she unwillingly gave in. She beat her pillows a few times and at the very least that small act of violent behavior made her feel she accomplished something. Regardless, the storm had won.

Looking around her bedroom, her animals made her smile. They needed her love and protection and it was nice to feel needed. The empty nest syndrome was never an issue. As Summer threw off her bed sheets and down comforter, she looked out her bedroom window at the approaching fury of a storm. Oh how the General loved to watch the storms from the rocks at Little Round Top. Being a ghost he never had to worry about getting struck by lightning, something Summer Ray was almost jealous of.

With flashes and crackling of electric blue, the thunderous clapping overhead, and the hallowing of the wind with hail smacking mercilessly into her windows, Summer's thoughts drifted to Savannah were the General was now held captive by that depraved and hideous fire witch Madeline. Summer's brief visit to her birthplace the year before, the charm and architecture of Historical Savannah, such picturesque beauty she knew she never would forget. Eventually, Summer would have to return to face Madeline, once she was reunited with her twin brother Anthony.

Savannah was founded in 1733 by General James Oglethorpe. He along with 113 men, women and children, sailed aboard the two hundred ton galley ship called "Anne." It landed on a high bluff parallel to the Savannah River. The bluff was called "Yamacraw Bluff" by the local Creek Indians. Greeting the settlers were Chief Tomo-chi-chi and his wife Senauki. The land was named "Georgia" after King George II of England and it became the thirteenth colony.

In 1778, Savannah during the Revolutionary War was recaptured by British Troops. It wasn't until the year 1782 the city was freed. Less than a 100 years later, January 1861,

Georgia became the fifth state to secede from the Union. Miraculously, Union General William T. Sherman on his famous "March to the Sea" spared the city of Savannah from being burnt and destroyed. His March began in May of 1864 in Chattanooga, then Atlanta, then through Macon. Sherman's march had already left a 30 mile wide and 300 mile long path of utter destruction before he and his soldiers bordered Savannah. In December of 1864, Charles Green, offered Sherman the use of his rather illustrious mansion on Madison Square for his headquarters. This act of bravely and tenacity, quite possibly kept the city from being destroyed. Yet it was here, in Mr. Green's home the Union General Sherman wrote to President Lincoln:

> *"I beg to present you, as a Christmas gift, the city of Savannah, with one hundred and fifty guns, and plenty of ammunition, and also about 25,000 bales of cotton."*

The Green home Sherman had taken use of until February 1, 1865, just a few short months shy of the Confederate surrender in April. With such an amazing part of history, Summer was starting to enjoy her new southern heritage. Yet, her roots as usual, were still buried beneath Union soil. Her Yankee heart was too much a part of her. Her love for the Union was branded into her, and it was doubtful she would ever let that go. The war was over and Summer could fall in love with the South, without regret or disrespect to her own Union legacy.

Sixty Seven Minutes

Summer looked over at her clock radio and the time now said 11:47pm. Although the thought to sneak into Little Round Top to catch some pictures of the light show, was nitpicking her, she tried to brush it off as insane. No one was allowed in the park after it was closed and Summer Ray had great respect for the National Park Service. Yet, almost as if an intangible magnet was pulling her, she jumped out of bed, terrified of what she what about to do. By the time she would get to Little Round Top, it would be well after midnight. Summer would have to walk up there alone and in a downpour no less. She thought of taking two of her dogs, but couldn't take the risk of them barking and making noise. "Yeah right, what was I thinking? They are a bunch of scardy-cats." Summer had to laugh as her dogs were piled on her bed trembling.

Summer changed out of her sort of sexy two piece flannel pajama's to her black worn out jeans, a light blue v-neck t-shirt, and a black hooded rain jacket. She then patted all her animals on the head and kept most of her house lights on. After grabbing her camera equipment she threw what she could into a backpack, and a rare commodity – an umbrella! She then headed out into the storm toward her SUV. Though she lived only a mile from Little Round Top, she still needed to drive as close to the Top as possible, though due to the torrential downpour, she had to drive at a snail's pace. Her windshield wipers were on full speed and even then they could not keep up with the deluge. Turning left at the corner of Corbins BBQ and Grill, off of Taneytown Avenue, Summer was suddenly hungry for one of their amazing BBQ beef sandwiches. Luckily, she threw some healthy trail mix in her backpack. "Damn diet!!!" she thought.

Finally reaching her destination, with the gates closed, Summer had to park on one of the back roads and hike. Luckily, she did not pass any other vehicles, including the Park Ranger's who live on the battlefields. In her mind there was no justification for such, in her eyes, "crazy, stupid, dangerous and illegal" behavior.

As she stepped out of her SUV with lightning flashing overhead, and almost already drenched from the rain she quietly prayed, "Father God, this is probably the stupidest and most dangerous thing I have ever done. Please keep me safe and if at all possible, please don't let me get caught. There is a reason I need to be here. Thank You, In Jesus Name...Amen." After she opened her umbrella and with her back pack in toe, she began the trek up to Little Round Top.

Summer could see to the right of her, the statue of General Warren. She must have taken over a 1,000 pictures of him over the years, yet no two are the same. For some reason, General Warren has always been a beacon of light for Summer Ray. The boulder, the one his statue is erected on, is said to have been the same boulder he stood on while he was in battle. General Warren was Chief of Engineers of the Army of the Potomac. He led Union troops to the "High Ground" of Little Round Top on the 2nd day of battle, July 2, 1863. This brilliant move secured the Union Line, and as Confederate Soldiers were advancing up the slope of Little Round Top, they were pushed back or killed by the waiting Union cannons.

It was said that blood was poured out in puddles on the rocks and that every square inch of the hill, as the dead or dying lay spewed across it.

Colonel William C. Oates of the 15th Alabama stated:

> *"My dead and wounded were nearly as great in number as those still on duty. They literally covered the ground.*
>
> *The blood stood in puddles in some places on the rocks; the ground was soaked with the blood of as brave men as ever fell on the red field of battle."*

Summer shivered at the thought of those dying men and the puddles of blood. Somehow the lightning and the time of night only exaggerated their suffering and frightened her even more, which it would do to most humans. Yet, not one to back down, she continued on. As much as she wanted to capture a picture of the General Warren in this billowing atmosphere, she didn't dare go near those boulders in this kind of weather. That was a death sentence for sure. Her aim was the castle and she stayed on the road until she reached the dirt path that lead straight up to the castle. Slipping on the mud soaked rocky path and tripping over broken limbs and roots from nearby trees, Summer knew she had to get a grip, or quite possibly break something or get struck by lightning. As she finally made her way through more briars, once she reached the top of the dirt path, she saw the gravel path lit up from the storm. Yet for fear of damaging her camera, she couldn't capture the reflection. Once safe and dry inside the castle walls, she could unpack her camera and equipment.

The castle stands 44 feet high and 12 feet wide. Those numbers are in reference to the Union 44th and 12th New York Volunteer Infantry Regiments who fought on that hill on July 2nd and July 3rd 1863. The castle also has winding spiral staircase that leads up to the 2nd floor observation deck. The tower is crowned with a Maltese Cross and characterizes the Fifth Army Corps and unlike the Lutheran Seminary cupola, the one Buford used to observe the location of the Confederate Army, this tower is not accessible as it is not open to the public.

The stone walls, exquisite architect, marble pillars and the arched doorways, one could not help but sense the past in the present. When lightning flashed before her, wow a breathtaking view it was. It lit up Gettysburg like an electric blue Christmas. Yet, Summer knew over 150 years prior, the rocky slopes, hills and boulders of Little Round Top and Devil's Den, were once covered with dead and dying soldiers. Yet, it wasn't something she could dwell on, at least not at the present moment.

So she unpacked her camera from her backpack, thankful both she and it were still safe. Though trembling from the storm, she was also terrified of the fact that she was alone, at least from a human standpoint, on Little Round Top after park hours. If she got hurt, no one would find her till morning. If she got caught by the NPS, she would be heavily fined, and quite possibly lose her privilege to take pictures on NPS property. But, it was already too late for rational thinking. She was where she was and wasn't about to leave until she captured the light show on film.

Standing in the door way facing Devil's Den, Summer could see the full moon above it. As streaks of lightning began to flash as far back in the horizon over South Mountain, Summer started snapping pictures. Awestruck at the beauty of what she was seeing, hearing the crack of lightning and the boom of thunder, it took her a few seconds to realize someone was standing behind her. Not knowing at first if that someone was human or not, her heart began to race a mile a minute. Summer was more afraid of the living than the dead. She didn't know if she should run out the castle door in front of her, but that would have meant she would have been blocked by the rain soaked rocks. Having broken her tail bone from a fall off of those slippery beasts once before, she was ever so hesitant to run in their direction. So, she chose to slowly turn around instead, in hopes her senses were playing tricks on her.

As she turned toward the other castle doorway directly behind her, stood this figure of Union General, silhouetted as light flashed behind him. His stature practically reached the top of the arch. As terror engulfed Summer, she turned back around and as she was about to make her escape, he shouted out, "Summer stop!"

Shell shocked that this stranger knew her name, from outside the castle wall she peeked back in the doorway and recognized him. As lightning flashed in the distance behind her, with her long hair dripping wet, with rain flowing down her face, Summer didn't realize how innocent and desirable she appeared to him. Thinking she looked like a drown rat, she hesitated to walk back inside, under the protection of the castle walls. Reluctantly she did. The backpack with her camera was there, or so she reasoned with herself. She slowly walked back up the steps to where he was standing inside the castle when she spoke in a broken voice, "What are you doing here and why are you dressed like that?"

The man answered, "I was just about to ask you that same question. But I was going to add, 'What the *hell* are you doing here?"

Summer replied, "Sorry! When I saw you, you scared the hell right out of me."

The man looked down at his clothes, grinned then said, "In regard to your second question, clothes are generally a requirement these days."

Summer took another look, confused she answered, "Oh! When the lightning burst through the archway, you looked like a Union General."

He replied, "I will take that as a compliment."

Summer wanted answers and asked again, "But seriously, what are you doing here?"

He replied, "Most nights when I can't sleep, I come up here. It tends to clear my head. But you are the first person I actually almost scared half to death. For a second there, I thought I was going to have to peel you off those boulders. You... out on a night like this, have you completely lost your mind? Not that I don't find it somewhat attractive. You, breaking park rules and all? It's almost…hot!"

Summer angrily replied, "Bite me!" It was unfair at how he could see right through her rain soaked skin, straight to her broken heart. She hadn't been that close to him in years. Yet, frozen in time, at that moment it felt to her like it was just yesterday. He still had that same dizzying affect on her. As he moved closer to her, she moved closer to the opposite doorway. Noticing how nervous she was, he smiled and said, "I am not going to hurt you."

Summer whispered, "No! You already did that."

In his defense he spoke, "Summer Ray, you were that last person I expected to find up here. You know, I don't believe in God the way you do. But this is almost divine." When he reached out to hold her, Summer's insides were melting all over again. Time hadn't healed her wrecked heart, nor had it erased the love she carried for him. He never knew it either, at least not until this moment. Alone in the castle, during a beautiful thunderstorm, just her and him, it was almost magical. Summer was trembling and she wasn't sure if it was due to his touch, or perhaps the wind against her rain soaked clothes had started to chill her to the bone.

    Summer abruptly pulled away from him and said, "I have to go. I don't want to catch pneumonia." When she walked over and bent down to pick up her backpack, he crouched down next to her and now with both hands holding her, he kissed her hard. Struggling to stop him, she finally gave in and grabbed on to him as tight as she could. The force of their passion caused both of them to crash to the castle floor. But she didn't care. This was her dream and she wasn't about to let go of it either. Her clothes were dripping wet not only from the rain, but also from her desire of this man she thought she would never see again. This man, who Summer believed at one time that God brought them together - a match made in Heaven. It was almost funny and cruel at the same time that he didn't believe in her God or any god for that matter!

The lightning blazed and the souls of this man and this woman were electrified by the inferno of their passion. The thunder roared all around them, but the booms were drowned out by the reverberation and beating of their conjoined bodies. They were like a tender vine attaching its roots to a tree, suctioning itself to the bark, and after awhile overtaking and becoming one with its branches. It was symbolic of what Jesus said in John 15:5, *"I am the vine, ye are the branches. If you remain in me and I in you, you will bear much fruit. For apart from me you can do nothing."* Oh how Summer wanted to remain with the love of her life, and be in Jesus at the same time. Yet, this man was an atheist. So how could she stay forever with a man who did not believe in the God she adored? If tonight was a test, she was failing miserably. She could only hope her God would understand.

Soldiers of the American Civil War, both Union and Confederate, some 150 years prior saw nothing but an endless wave of death and destruction, from the hill these two lovers were now enjoying. The soldiers were never far from Summer's thoughts and she almost felt a sense of guilt. But, this was now and that was then. Summer drifted into a world she never knew existed and could hardly believe she was sharing it with him. Not knowing what tomorrow morning would bring, for the next few seconds, minutes or hours, she would simply cherish every bit of it, loving him once again.

CHAPTER NINE

Reality

As usual, Summer's alarm clock echoed an annoying chime of "beep, beep, beep," at precisely 6:00 in the morning. Startled by its sound, Summer shook herself awake. Frantic that she woke up in her own bed and not on Little Round Top, she desperately tried to remember the previous early morning hours. She threw off her plush light blue quilt, noticing there were not any of her animals at her bedside. When she left the night before, in the thunderstorm, they had all piled onto her bed like scared little rabbits and not the brave German shepherds and Border Collie she is so proud of. The cats even risked the dogs' wrath of their infringement on what the dogs believed were their own private property... the bed. But, nonetheless, the cats took advantage of their fright. It was after all a hellacious storm that had marched into town. It was as if another war was fast approaching, with soldiers on foot and on horseback as thousands of hooves rumbled and roared as they made their way across the landscape.

Summer anxious for answers, ran downstairs to retrieve her camera out of her backpack. Yet, she found it on the table and the battery was safely attached to its charger. Summer thought, "I don't remember charging the battery when I got home." She took the battery of the charger and snapped it into her camera and turned it on. Sitting now at her kitchen table, Summer began to examine the pictures she took at Little Round Top the night before. To her dismay, there were no pictures of the storm. Knowing she took at least 100 of them Summer tried to put the pieces together. She then noticed her flannel pajamas and ran back up to her bedroom to see where she left her wet clothes. Summer was never really one for neatness, usually things ended up on the floor, or thrown half way into the laundry basket. Upon reaching her bedroom, the clothes she wore the night before were not spewed about her bedroom, nor where they in the adjoining bathroom. With a now sunken heart, she opened up her dresser drawers and found the clothes she was wearing all tucked away nice and neat. This prompted her to run back down stairs again to the coat closet. Summer was much too lazy to wipe off a dripping wet coat and wouldn't dare hang it next to her prized leather jackets. Yet, as she opened the closet door, there it was. Her tan rain coat was hanging up as if it hadn't been worn.

Summer went into her living room, switched on the lights and fell onto the rocking chair and said, "That couldn't have been a dream. He was there, I know it. We both were." Looking outside the bay windows, she saw enough of the sun coming up. The castle in about 20 minutes would be her destination. But first, she had to let the dogs out and feed her brood of animals. The clock now read 6:23am. When Summer called the dogs back inside, she noticed that the grass wasn't wet. The mist and fog that usually hovers the ground and the mountains, wasn't there either. The thought the night before was nothing but a dream, instantly tore through Summer's soul as if a cannonball had just exploded right in front of it.

    The drive to Little Round Top, though anxious, it seemed like a slow crawl at a snail's pace. Summer didn't want to find what she knew she was going to...nothing! As an experienced Gettysburg photographer she instinctively knew, if it had stormed there would be evidence such as debris of twigs, leaves and white dogwood petals, puddles of water, mist and fog. Yet, her convictions were right. There wasn't a trace a thunderstorm had viciously plowed through the town. The area echoed a silent and serene calm. The birds were chirping like they always do. The sun was just starting to crest over the top of the castle and Summer was grief stricken. She walked inside the archway and looked through it to Devil's Den. A tear or two started to trickle down her face. The other sound of, "it was only a dream" rang loud and clear inside her heart and head.

As Summer turned around to leave, the sun had managed to beam right through both archways of the castle onto the nearby rocks and boulders. Something that was shining had caught Summer's attention. Her curiosity wasn't about to let her overlook it. Carefully, she had to climb up and down a few rocks to take a closer look. Dumbfounded, she saw the object. It was the Colonel Marsh's pocket watch. Summer said, "What the..." She picked it up, and shrieked when she saw that it now read, "4:07." The last time it ticked and stopped was when her and Kat came back from finding her twin brother during the Civil War. The time then read "3:00." Sixty seven minutes the pocket watch had ticked. An early morning drive to her grandmother's and the Gatekeeper's house was in the immediate, right now, future!

Own Little World

Luckily, the Gatekeeper was already walking around the National Cemetery and the Shaman was making coffee and cinnamons rolls. When the Gatekeeper saw Summer's SUV pull into the driveway, he started the long walk back toward his home. He needed to see what was going on at this early morning hour. Both he and his wife knew, Summer usually was out taking pictures of the sunrise and normally doesn't call them until after 9:00AM.

The Shaman greeted Summer at the door. Before her grandmother could get a word in edgewise, Summer exclaimed, "Look at this watch grandmother. The time went from 3:00 to 4:07. Sixty seven minutes went by. Why and how did it do that? I thought it didn't tick in our time."

"Anastasia," her grandmother said, then asked, "Where were you this morning?" Summer put her head down and answered, "I thought I was on Little Round Top in the castle taking pictures of the storm." Already knowing the answer the Shaman asked, "And were you alone?" Summer blushed then said, "I am not sure. I took over a 100 pictures last night of the storm and there isn't a trace of them on my camera. There isn't a trace of him either."

As the Shaman poured Summer's coffee, she said, "But the watch, it was ticking, or at least it is showing now that it had started to tick and then stopped."

Summer was trying to figure out what was going on when the Gatekeeper stepped in and offered to help her. "The reason the pictures did not develop is simple. During the Civil War that camera had not been invented yet. As for the man, he is your heart's desire Summer Ray and he always has been."

The Shaman asked, "Did you recognize him?"

Summer answered, "Yes ma-am. He even held me. He said he couldn't sleep and felt he needed to go to the castle. But wait, you said," looking at the Gatekeeper, "during the Civil War that camera had not been invented yet. So was last night another trip back in time? Is that why the watch had stopped ticking at 4:07?"

The Gatekeeper asked, "Who is the man Summer Ray?"

Summer replied, "I would rather not say."

The Shaman answered for her, "It was Sam." Looking at her grand-daughter she asked, "Am I right?" Summer though hesitant to answer finally did, "Yes! Grandmother it was him. But he probably doesn't even know it."

The Gatekeeper inquired, "Who is Sam?"

A distraught Summer Ray looked at him and began to spill the painful memories of when she first met him and how she fell head over teacups for him. She informed the Gatekeeper,

"Well I guess it's been close now to eighteen years ago when Kat and I first came back to Gettysburg. It was right after I had that ballroom dream where the General McDaniels told me to remember my promise. When Kat and I went ghost hunting for the General, I saw a bookstore sign on Steinwehr. I know it sounds crazy. But from what I can remember, it looked like the sign had an aura around it. I knew I needed to go inside." Summer laughed as she remembered the next part and continued, "It was really funny. I tripped in the foyer and I felt like I was in another time. It was really weird. But, then I took that step into the entrance to the bookstore and there he was behind the counter. Somehow time stood still and yet, it almost knocked me over at the same time. He followed me to the back of the store where I was looking books." Summer sighed and then looked out the bay window and spoke, "I have never felt so perfect in all my life."

The Gatekeeper sat down on a chair beside Summer Ray and looked sadly into her eyes and informed her, "Oh that Sam. I have known him for years. I just never knew how you felt about him. But, he left town about six months ago."

Summer not believing the sting of his words asked, "What?"

The Gatekeeper continued, "I went into the bookstore he worked at and I was told by his boss that he left Gettysburg back in May."

The Shaman responded, "You have been in your own little world, oblivious to what was happening around you. But are you aware my dear that you can remember every little detail about your encounter with Sam and yet, you cannot remember what you had for breakfast?"

Summer after giving her grandmother a strange look asked the Gatekeeper, "Did his boss say where he went?"

He replied, "I didn't ask. But if you would like, I will this afternoon."

Summer jumped to her feet and exclaimed, "No! I don't want to interfere. If he is happy, I need to let him go and be happy for him."

The Shaman stepped in, "How do you know he is happy, if he came back here for you?" Summer was silent. The Gatekeeper asked, "Would Sam be a Union or Confederate?" Summer quickly answered, "Union."

As if unwinding the tapes, the Gatekeeper continued, "You had a dream that you were in Charleston. You said your husband died in Gettysburg and that a Union General came to visit you. Do you have any recollection as to what he looked like?"

The Shaman interjected, "Summer you MUST remember what he looked like. If you cannot remember on your own, I will bring out the tea leaves."

Summer dreading the thought of having to remember something through witchcraft, would have to seriously think and think hard. She had almost forgotten about that dream. But it is also the same dream where she named her granddaughter Serenity Hope.

Summer stated, "Serenity" was the name of the homestead we lived at. I was Anastasia Adams. The Union General told me my husband died here in Gettysburg."

Summer saddened continued, "We are back to square one and really don't know any more than we did."

The Shaman assured her grand-daughter, "Of course we do! We must get you back to Charleston. You, my dear, need to keep that General around. We need to know who he is. If he is your Sam, it would explain why the pocket watch ticked when the two of you were…shall I say, TOGETHER!"

Summer, too numb to speak her only reply was, "Yes ma-am."

A dejected Summer Ray left the Gatekeeper and her grandmother and drove her car straight to Sach's Covered Bridge. God promised her that she wouldn't be crushed again. The emotions she felt about Sam leaving town were a rude awakening for her. The night she sort of spent with him at the castle, reality or dream she wasn't about to dismiss it.

    Sitting on the banks of Marsh Creek as the sun was reflecting off the water and bridge, her Guardian Angel Rory and Warrior Angel Sostar were sitting on top of the bridge. Though the temperature was in the mid 40's, Summer didn't mind the cold. She just wrapped herself tighter with the blanket she took out of her car and stared into the reflection of the bridge in the water. Summer, alone in her thoughts, was unaccompanied in a human sense. She didn't notice the Angels on top of the bridge nor of the sinister spirits lurking at her through the woods across the water. Some ghost people have come running out of those woods, scared to almost death that they have seen a "portal to the other side." The Sach's Covered Bridge is notorious place for frightening the day lights out of people. Yet for Summer Ray Sherwood, it is a sanctuary of Light and peace. As Summer was soul searching she took out her notepad from her backpack and began to write:

NOW I KNOW

It seems we are worlds apart,
Now I know it's true.
Yet forever here inside my heart,
There's still me and you.

You left without saying, "Goodbye."
I didn't know how or when.
I am too numb to even cry,
Will I ever see you again?

It feels like a hole has been punched through my chest,
My soul how it does ache.
Maybe I should let love rest,
So that my heart again won't break.

But since when did that do anyone good,
Taking the easy way out of love?
If only I thought that I could,
But you are all that I dream of.

Now I know finally this much is true,
I am lost, without the hope of tomorrow.
When I could really be with you,
Not stuck in a past of sorrow.

While reaching for the stars, somehow did I,
Miss what mattered along the way?
I never bothered to even try,
So many words I failed to say.

So I will say them now, just so you know,
That now I know, I need you with me.
I love you, though I let you go,
If you turn around, here for you I'll be!

While reaching for the stars, somehow did I,
　　Miss what mattered along the way?
　　　I never bothered to even try,
　　　So many words I failed to say.

So I will say them now, just so you know,
　　That now I know, I need you with me.
　　　I love you, though I let you go,
　　　If you turn around, here for you I'll be!

Though not sure of the how's or when's in regard to Sam, she knew she HAD to see him again. But, she also knew she HAD to free the General and the Colonel Marsh from the bonds that held them. Finding Sam would have to wait. Summer with her new found hope, only hope that by the time she did find him, it wouldn't be too late. She knew God had ALL the answers and she also knew He would reveal them in His time and not in hers. At least He made Summer Ray aware her true feelings. Without any shadow of any doubt, she was hopelessly in love with Sam. The journey home for the General Michael Moses McDaniels, the Union Lt. Colonel Jameson, the Confederate Cololnel JD Marsh and the Unknowns, Summer could only hope that their final destiny, meant the beginning of a new one for her and Sam.

After all, how could she love a ghost? How could she spend the rest of her life joined to a spirit and not to human flesh? The General couldn't be a real man to Summer Ray, could he? She would always have to keep him hidden. Who was she kidding? She was failing miserably at trying to justify her heart. At age 52, Summer's life was already half over. The seconds turned rapidly into hours and hours turned even quicker into days. Pretty soon, months and then years would fly by. Summer was empty without Sam and he was unaware of her longing for him. Was it even fair not to tell him? Would he have even left town if he knew Summer loved him so much? Maybe he felt he had nothing left to stay for. Would he have made different choices if he really knew that love was also within his reach? Would he find the comfort he was so desperately seeking in her arms?

Still, so many unanswered questions that only time could speak of. Even with ten roads that lead into Gettysburg, there wasn't one that could lead her to Sam. She didn't even know where he was or which road to follow. So, she simply had to follow her heart. Anthony had to be found. If there was ever any hope of a future with Sam, her twin brother HAD to be found first.

CHAPTER TEN

Battle Scars

The next day, the Shaman called her granddaughter to arrange an emergency meeting. The Shaman told Summer she had some new leads on Anthony's whereabouts. The December snow had started to fall. Summer was decorating her new home for its first Christmas with her and her growing family. Finally, she was exited. Serenity Hope, a beautiful 8 pound and 3 ounce baby girl was born on December 3rd, the same day as Summer Ray's father. Yes the circle and cycle of life was indeed turning.

Summer told her grandmother she would be at her house by noon. With the snow slightly sticking to the pavement, Summer did not want her grandmother and the Gatekeeper out in these weather conditions. When Summer tried to reach Kat, she couldn't. It was almost an impossibility as the two them were like Jonathan and David attached to each other's hip. To Summer's surprise, her best friend was already waiting for her at the Gatekeeper's house.

Summer didn't stop for hello's when she ordered, "Okay what is going on? Kat you always answer your phone. Why didn't you tell me you were coming?" The Shaman already suspected Summer had a feeling what the two of them had done. Summer confirmed her grandmother's suspicions when she blurted out, "Damnit! I told you both I did not want to find Anthony through witchcraft. What the hell did you two do?"

Kat replied, "Summer Ray calm down. It was the only way and it did not involve you."

The Shaman answered, "My dear child, this is not just about you. Sometimes you just have to allow other people the right to make their own decisions."

Summer still angry shouted, "Do you know how many demons you opened the door for grandmother? And Kat, what were you thinking?"

Kat walked over to her friend and stated, "Listen to what your grandmother just said. Sometimes you just have to allow other people to make their own decisions."

Summer slumped down on the black leather recliner and said, "I am sorry. I am almost afraid to ask, but what did you find out?" Kat answered, "Summer, there are some things I never told you. Things, I thought insignificant, where obviously clues that I never picked up on."

Summer inquired, "What clues?"

Kat sat down on a barstool and began to explain. When you were on the ice at the Rockefeller Center, I was standing at rink side. A man, who resembled the Major Benjamin, came and stood beside me. He asked who you were and sadly, I blew him off. I didn't want him to interrupt your moment on the ice. I did manage to find out that he was also a skater. But, that is all the information I have."

The Shaman stepped in, "We also found out he is a New York City Firefighter."

Summer gasped, "What? Do you know what company? Wouldn't he be almost retired by now?" Summer put her head down as a memory flashed through her eyes. She perked up and looked at Kat and asked, "Kat, do you remember before Tommy and I got married, long before we started to even date, we went to Rescue 3 in the Bronx. I was one of the first women to ride on the new rig. We responded to a few fires and Tommy and I even spent the firehouse a few times. This is so weird. We both skate. We both were in the fire service. I wonder if he likes history."

The Shaman added, "He must or you wouldn't have been able to find him." Kat and the Shaman looked at each other, and then the Gatekeeper asked, "Do either you two young ladies have any clues that might help you locate Anthony from your time travel?"

Summer looked at him with a blank stare and with squinted eyes, she said, "I need Kat to help me remember." Then pointing to the scar on her neck she sarcastically continued, "Oh that's right! He tried to slit my throat, but left me this little souvenir instead."

Kat interjected, "Battle scars, Summer Ray, battle scars!" Then she stood up and walked around the room. The Shaman and her husband and Summer Ray were all watching silently, as if watching a home movie being projected from Kat's thoughts. The Gatekeeper asked, "Do you recollect any names that may have stood out?"

Kat answered, "Well, his name was Major Bryce Alexander Benjamin."

The Shaman inquired, "Summer Ray, did you ever do research on that name?"

Summer shook her head, "No! I am sorry grandmother. If you recall when I came back from Savannah, I was somewhat emotionally distraught by the General's rather harsh dismissal of me."

The Gatekeeper slowly walked over to his computer as the three ladies patiently waited. He pulled up Google and ran Anthony's Confederate name in the search engine. Oddly enough, there was no one in the Confederacy by that name. He walked over to his massive Civil War library and also looked through his many war books on roll calls and enlistees. The Major Bryce Alexander Benjamin's name was absent. A dumbfounded Summer asked, "Just what is that supposed to mean? Does he, or does he not exist?"

The Shaman, quite possibly guessing stated, "You are not known in that time period either Anastasia. There are some things that I cannot explain. But, just because they are un-explainable, it does not make void the facts. The fact is you and Anthony met at some camp in the Civil War in Tennessee, am I correct?"

The Gatekeeper asked, "Do either of you remember the name of that camp?"

Kat responded faster than Summer Ray, "Yes, it was Camp Trousdale. It was a horrific place to be. I know I will never forget the condition of that camp or those suffering soldiers."

Summer repeated the name, "Trousdale" over and over again and then suddenly jumped to her feet. She asked the Gatekeeper if she could research 'Anthony Trousdale' on the computer. When Firefighter Tony Trousdale of FDNY appeared in the search engine, Summer screamed for Kat, "Kat, look at this. Is this the man you saw?"

Kat did more than just look. Her heart had that strange yet peaceful feeling it had, when she first encountered him at the Rockefeller Center.

Kat admonished, "Wow! He is some kind of gorgeous." Summer laughed, "First it was David Lee of SwampdaWamp and now it's my twin brother?"

Kat replied, "Well David is happily married. I just hope your long lost infamous twin isn't. That would almost kind a suck!"

Summer looked at her friend and said, "Not sure I could handle you as a sister in law."

The Shaman finally walked over to the computer to get a good look at her grandson Anthony. What was stolen from her long ago, was finally being restored. Her daughter, the twin's mother, would never be replaced. But at least the two babes are alive and well and about to be re-united.

Summer asked, "So what do we do now? New York City is awfully huge grandmother. It won't be so easy as it was when Kat and I ran into you."

The Shaman answered, "It was the ice that brought him to you. It will be the ice again. We all will be at the Rockefeller Center on Christmas Eve. Summer Ray, you need to tell Billy and Emma as they need to be a part of this."

The Shaman gave out the marching orders as to who would be doing what in New York City at Christmas. This was a family affair and all would be present to find their beloved Anthony.

CHAPTER ELEVEN

Past & Present

Manhattan, New York City

Tony Trousdale was not only a retired FDNY Firefighter, he was also a retired Rangers Ice Hockey Player. Countless of times Summer Ray watched the Rangers games. Tony's hair was also coal black like his twin sister. His eye color was a light green. Where Summer's is a lighter brown with green mixed in. Tony's height was 6' 2" just like his nephew Billy. Summer's twin was divorced and his son's name is Tyler Trousdale, a travelling musician.

Tony became a firefighter at a very young age, eighteen to be exact. He grew up in Kentucky. His adopted father was an Engineer on the Union Pacific Railroad. Tony's adopted mother was a hairstylist and owned her own salon. Tony's parents are both in their late 70's and still living in Louisville, Kentucky. Tony grew up without siblings. He knew he was adopted and though time and time again he tried to find his biological parents, he never could. His birth certificate was altered like his twin sister's Summer Ray and both stated they were "single births."

Louisville, where Tony lived the first twenty five years of his life, he was also an experienced equestrian. His parents owned a few races horses. But, their breed was not that of Kentucky Derby quality. The ranch he grew up on, Tony learned to rope and ride, play the guitar, sing and was an expert sharpshooter. He had several serious relationships with the local cowgirls in town. But his love for the big city, ice and fire, he left home and moved to Manhattan. At first, he was like a fish out of water. But, like fish, he learned to adapt to his surroundings. Tony also learned the North was very different from the South in its culture.

The Big Apple, during pre war time, was a rather large import of cotton. Though against slavery, they traded with the South who used slaves to work the cotton plantations. This economic practice gave the name "contradiction" a whole new level of definition. If they were so against slavery, why would they have traded with the South that wasn't? It was little details like this that caused Summer Ray to take one step closer to her Southern heritage. Clearly, the Civil War was not a slave issue. It was rather a political issue over power. New York City was a port to both the North and the South. Business had boomed. The town was thriving when the Civil War came into fruition.

The New York City draft riots of 1863 damn near destroyed the city and almost won the war for the Confederacy. The riots took place just two weeks after the Battle of Gettysburg where close to 30,000 New Yorkers were killed, wounded or missing. Many black men were found hanged from lampposts, as black orphaned children ran into the streets of chaos after their orphanages were torched. Those who supported Lincoln also found themselves either beaten or were forced to watch as rioters burnt their homes and livelihoods burnt as well. Churches, especially black ones and city parks were also set on fire. Union soldiers sent to protect the city were killed by raging civilians. Had the rioters prevailed, some believed that most definitely the South would have won the Civil War for sure!

CHAPTER TWELVE

Her Handkerchief

The winter of 1867 in Charleston, South Carolina was indeed a brutal one. The bitter cold left its mark on three of Anastasia's slaves, who died of pneumonia. She appealed to the South Carolina war department for help. But, until the South could be restored, no help was to be given. She was left to fend for herself. Yet, her nearest neighbor Mrs. Millie Lake, a 38 year old widow like herself was Anastasia's closest friend. The two ladies would meet with other widows every Tuesday to sew and mostly gossip. Though a Christian, Anastasia had to admit the gossip kept her mind off other things.

One particular Tuesday afternoon proved to be quite informative for Ms. Anastasia Adams. Corine Collins, who owns and operates a bed and breakfast from her home, finally spilled the beans to the ladies in the group, of this handsome

Yankee General who always comes to town at least once a month. Anastasia put her tea cup on the saucer and pretended not to be too interested and yet kept a close ear. Anastasia would never admit to missing her handsome stranger who tried to help her with Serenity awhile back. Her Southern Pride never allowed her to confess such horrific tidings. He, after all, was the reason her beloved husband was killed in Gettysburg. Forgiveness only carried her so far, until the memories showed up.

Yet she was curious as to who this Yankee General was. Millie, knowing Anastasia's secret, seeing her friend so bashful stepped in and asked for her, "Does this General have a name? What does he look like?" Corine exclaimed, "Oh Millie, he is to die for! His eyes are baby blue like the sky. His smile with those dimples, oh I could just eat him all up!"

Millie asked, "What does he want? Does he ever tell you?"

Corine responded as she was sewing flowers on a napkin, "Well no, not exactly! I even tried to give him my handkerchief and he politely refused. He said he already had one and that it smelled like honeysuckle and roses."

Anastasia almost choked on Corine's last statement and coughed up some of her tea onto her day dress. The ladies gasped, "Anastasia darling, are you alright?"

Barely able to get the words out she wailed, "Oh I beg your pardon. I am so sorry."

Corine responded, "He comes to town alone carrying a woman's handkerchief. You know who ever it belongs to, he must be grieving for."

An overly zealous Millie stated, "Well then, we can't have a Yankee General all lonesome, now can we ladies? We must have a ball to meet this poor General. Don't you think so? It is time we accept our defeat in admiration and have a ball in honor of the true nature of South Carolina. We are a gracious and proud people, are we not? Have we not all finished mourning our beloveds? Is it not time we dance and restore not only our beloved South but our own lives as well?"

As the other ladies agreed, brain stormed, laughed and frolicked at the thought of a ball, Anastasia Adams was on to her best friend's scheme. She asked, "What are you doing? You know I have nothing to wear to this ball?"

Millie pulled a fast one, "Ladies, we must make Anastasia the belle of the ball. We need to make her a gown."

Anastasia chimed in, "Oh no! You know Serenity is barely able to sustain us as it is. I could never take from it to purchase a new gown. I just couldn't."

The room fell silent when the Matron Laurise stood a mere 5 feet and 1 inch, onto her wobbled feet and spoke, "My dear Ana, how long will you continue to mourn and feel sorry for yourself? A young woman such as yourself must not spend her life alone. It is not proper. Though you are widowed, you must find a new husband. You must have children. Who will you leave Serenity to? Your slaves?"

When the Matron spoke and barked out orders, there was no denying them. Anastasia was going to this ball whether she liked it or not. Yet, a twinge of joy sparked inside her. She knew this General held her handkerchief. If the other ladies knew that, oh how they would turn green with envy. It will be a sight Anastasia would love to see, as some of these high society ladies, are truly and overbearingly shallow. Yet the Rules of Engagement were written in stone. Union and Confederate officers and soldiers as well as civilian men would be invited, along with every other female within a 100 mile radius. Millie whispered to Anastasia, "If he kept your handkerchief, you must mean something to him."

Anastasia after saying her goodbyes to the other ladies, as she was walking out the door replied to Millie, "If I meant so much, why didn't he come back all winter? Three of my slaves died and the rest of us almost starved."

Millie answered, "I don't know. But from the sound of things, he never really left."

A Rude Awakening

Kyly came up to his mistress Anastasia and asked, "Are you ready Miss Anastasia, I have the buckboard right over there?" Kyly pointed to an old worn out carriage. The horse attached to the buckboard was a thoroughbred named, "Skylar." Next to Serenity, he was Anastasia's prized possession. He was her husbands' horse and every morning before the war, the two of them would get up and ride for hours. They wanted children. But decided it would be best to wait until after the war was over.

Armistead perhaps knew in the back of his mind that he wasn't coming home to be a father.

He didn't want to leave his beloved wife a widow and a single parent at the same time. Still Anastasia yearned for a part of him. It was undeniably sad the horse was the only part. When the Yankee's tried to steal him, Anastasia without any dignity left in her, begged the Union soldier who held Sylar's reigns to please let her keep her husband's horse. When he dropped the reigns and rode off, Anastasia fell to the ground, beating it hysterically. She was a sight of so many a shattered people in both the North and in the South. Such a stupid war that never gave the South what they wanted, their freedom!

Ana held out her hand to Kyly, smiled and said, "Yes Kyly. I am ready." As she kept her hand on his, a few gasps could be heard in the background. Slaves were free, yet to some they were still not equals. Kyly was the son of her slave Daisy who died over the winter. Daisy was forty three and became ill when an outbreak of pneumonia reached Serenity. Anastasia vowed to her friend that she would look after Kyly. At 17, Kyly was already quite learned in reading and writing and would soon be able to work for a local newspaper. When Doc Jones came to Serenity, Anastasia was told his services were already taken care of and not to worry about how to pay him.

Yet, even with all of his wonderful efforts, Daisy, Arny & Donny, succumbed to that horrible plague. A frail Anastasia refused to leave their side. As their fevers spiked, her cool washcloths were a minimal source of comfort. Daisy, knowing her time drew near, clutched her mistress by the hand and pleaded with her to take care of her boy. Anastasia then grabbed Kyly's hand and assured her dying friend when she told her, "Yes Daisy. I will forever." With that, Daisy breathed her last and died in the arms of her mistress. The good doctor did all that he could do.

It dawned on Anastasia that she never bothered to inquire about who paid for his services. So turned to Kyly and said, "Wait here. I will be right back."

Kyly stated, "Yes ma-am." When Millie saw her friend walk toward Liberty Street, she caught up to her and asked, "Where are you going Ana?"

Anastasia answered, "To see Doc Jones. I have to ask him something."

Millie couldn't resist the curiosity of it all and went along with her.

The General Store was next to the doctor's office. As carriages and horses were passing the ladies, dirt flew up like smoke. Anastasia never replaced her handkerchief. So out of her ridicule, Millie pulled out hers to help brush the dirt off from both her and her friend. Once inside the doctor's office, Anastasia spoke to the assistant, the doctor's wife of fifty years.

"Hello Mrs. Jones. Please, is the doctor in? I need to see him." she said.

Mrs. Jones answered, "Yes Anastasia. What is the problem are you sick?"

Anastasia replied, "No ma-am. But I really need to ask him something." Just then the elderly Mr. Jones, a doctor of forty years came out to greet her and Millie.

Mrs. Jones informed her husband, "Anastasia said she needed to ask you something and from the looks of her anxiety, it must be very important."

The Doctor asked, "What is it Ana?"

Anastasia pulled the good doctor to the side and said, "Over the winter, when you came to Serenity, you said that your services had already been paid for. Did you just make that up, or did someone pay you?"

Doc Jones put his hand on Ana's shoulders and informed her, "A Yankee General by the name of Garret Rodgers paid me."

Anastasia asked, "General Rodgers? Who is he? I have never heard of him."

The doctor informed a bewildered Ana, "He knows you Anastasia and your husband. He said you would kill him if he ever came back to Serenity. He wanted to pay a debt. But when he heard of the condition of your slaves, knowing how impoverished you were at the time, he paid my fees. Why do you ask?"

A stunned Anastasia only replied, "No reason. Thank you Doctor Jones, Mrs. Jones."

Millie grabbed her friend by the arm and led her back outside.

Anastasia angrily wailed, "I have to find him."

Millie inquired, "Are you going to shoot him like you promised?"

Anastasia answered, "I am not a charity case Millie." Millie responded, "No Ana you are not. But the General feels the need to help you based on the fact he is the reason your husband is dead."

Anastasia stopped short, "My husband is dead due to honor, not because of the General. He owes me nothing and I have to pay him back."

Millie grabbing her friend by the shoulders abruptly asked, "Why do you have to pay him back Ana? This stupid pride of yours is really getting old. Most of us would love to have a man like that in our corner. Yet you refuse to accept his acts of kindness."

Anastasia stormed back into Corine's Bed & Breakfast, found Corine and asked, "Do you have a Yankee General by the name of Garret Rodgers that stays here?"

Corine responded, "Yes Ana that is the gentlemen I spoke of today."

Anastasia asked, "Do you know when he will return." Corine bent down to look at the calendar on her desk, shuffled a few papers, adjusted the lighting and said, "He will be here a week from Saturday. That is the night I have just scheduled the ball. Why do you ask?"

Anastasia curtseyed and her only reply was, "Thank you Corine. I will see you next Tuesday."

Millie walked out behind her friend and asked, "Okay! What is going on in that head of yours. I can see the wheels turning from here. You know you cannot be rude to a Yankee General Ana, certainly not in a public place. We are women of breeding and deportment. You do not want to dishonor your beloved Southern heritage do you?"

Anastasia cautiously answered, "Of course not. But I refuse to be in debt to a Yank."

Millie drilled her friend, "The debt was not for you. Do you realize that? This has nothing to do with you. He wanted to help your slaves that were sick."

When Anastasia saw Kyly run up to her again, it did her heart good to see such a strapping growing young man. She knew his momma and poppa would have been proud. Kyly's dad was killed during the war. Anastasia often wondered if the slaves would have ever been set free, had the Civil War not had happened. Her husband would still be alive and her cherished home would not have been ravaged by Yankee bloodhounds. The South lost and whatever decision was made to secede, there was no turning back. Time could not be re-wound to April 12, 1861 when Confederate guns at Ft. Sumter opened fire on Federal enlisted men. Four years later and over 600,000 casualties was it worth it? The South was still part of the Union. Their President Jefferson Davis was confined to a Yankee prison. Truly time cannot be altered.

The Spirit of the South

The day for the ball was fast in approaching. The ladies had made Anastasia a most beautiful ball gown of hunter green taffeta adorned with lace. Her bare shoulders and cleavage due to her corset, the Matron Laurise made sure would gain the attention of suitors. Anastasia long black hair was curled and pulled up. A matching lace head piece was added with a few small roses. Pearls graced her petite neckline and Anastasia was thrilled to look like a real lady again. She was certain the General Rodgers would not even recognize her. Hundreds of South Carolinians attended the ball. It was the first one in over six months. Yet, it was long overdue.

Though the South was broken and torn in two, yet the spirit of the South and their souls and heritage lived on. The South would indeed rise again. Many a suitors came a calling to dance with Miss Anastasia. Yet, she refused every single one. The Matron Laurise was none too happy with the uncooperative Anastasia Adams. She huffed passed her as Millie came to her friend's rescue and asked, "What are you doing? You cannot refuse every man that asks you to dance. You know that Anastasia. You know you are causing a ruckus with the Matron." Just then a familiar General approached the two ladies. When

Anastasia saw him she thought she would faint. So much so she turned and ran out of the ballroom. The General not far behind finally caught up with her as she was leaving to go outside. General Rodgers stopped her short, "Where are you going Anastasia?"

Anastasia could barely look at him. Yet, this time it wasn't out of hate. She greatly admired him and wasn't about to let it show.

General Rodgers spoke, "Still running away I see?" Anastasia could no longer hide the truth her heart so desperately wanted to reveal. He looked like a statue of Stonewall Jackson so grand and perfect, yet the color of his uniform was Yankee blue. The General Rodgers had memorialized himself inside her and Anastasia felt like a traitor to the Cause for even wanting him. Though the war was over from a technical standpoint, to the South, it will never be over! "The South Will Rise Again," is that not what has echoed throughout the centuries?

Yet the blush on Anastasia's cheeks gave her away. The General bent down and kissed her without asking permission. For a split second she gave into him. She put her arms around his neck, her bosoms up to his chest and kissed him back. Anastasia was dreaming and did not want to wake up to the reality he was still her enemy. Frantic she pulled away from him. Her head was fuzzy from emotion and her body was all of the sudden electrified from his touch. Yet, her pride got the best of her. Filled with his own emotion he spoke, "I do not want to let you go Anastasia. Please do not make me leave you again. Let me help you."

Realizing what he just said, knowing she would take it the wrong way, tears welled up in her eyes and she defiantly yelled at him, "I am not a weak willed widow."

General Rodgers replied, "I know that Anastasia that is what I love about you. Can you not see that? I love you. I want you to marry me?"

Anastasia answered, "Why so it will remove the guilt you have for killing my husband?"

This time she knew she went too far. He simply reached into his pocket and threw down her handkerchief and walked away. As she started to cry hysterically she bent down to retrieve her husband's handkerchief. She was sadly torn with the reality that if she were to marry the General Rodgers, it would somehow mar her dead husband's good name. He was a Yankee for god's sake. The man her husband saluted right before a musket ball pierced through his side. He was dead within minutes of hitting the ground. How could she fall in love with a man such as this?

Yet, not wanting to lose the General, like a little girl she ran after him. The rain had started to fall and as she was running her hair came loose and fell around her shoulders. Wet from rain, muddy from the dirt road, but she did not care. She had to get to him before he reached his horse. Each second seemed like an eternity as he disappeared around Marion Square. She survived the war and the death of her husband. But nothing in her could guarantee she would still be standing, should she lose the love of this Yank.

Screaming as loud as she could, "General Rodgers where are you?" Passerby's saw her and wondered at the state of this young woman. Though thunder and lightning echoed all around her, she wasn't about to stop running. As he mounted his horse he saw her running toward him. This crazy rain soaked woman who desperately needed him. But, as the thundered roared over head, the General's horse reared up and scaring Anastasia she tripped and fell face first onto the dirt. The General managed to steer his horse away from her as he jumped off and ran to her. Half unconscious she lay and he begged God to not let her die. With one swift movement he rolled her over into his arms.

"Anastasia!" he wailed. The sight of her brokenness was too much for him to bear. As his tears fell across her face, somehow she could differentiate them from the rain. She lifted her right arm around his neck and he buried his face in her neck and hair. Time briefly stopped for these two lovers. He lifted her into his arms, saddled his horse with her in front of him and rode off into the stormy night. Not knowing where he was taking her, but she did not care. She was with him and that was all that mattered. Anastasia leaned back against his chest and trusted that love would take here where ever it wanted her to go.

CHAPTER THIRTEEN

A Sign

It was Christmas Eve for both the North and the South. The Bonaventure Cemetery, for the first time in a very long time, snow instead of fog had blanketed the sacred ground. The monuments, partly covered in snow, gave off a fresh new admiration for such beauty. The General Michael Moses McDaniels, couldn't help but notice the unusual snowfall. Back in his beloved Gettysburg, he knew there must be snow on the blighted landscape up there. But here? No! There was something more going on. The General's rage after thinking Summer Ray only loved him due to some silly spell the witch put on a pocket watch, turned into sincere heartfelt longing for her. Oh how he missed her. He knew once again, he had hurt her even more than the last time.

The Colonel Marsh spoke up, "This snowfall Sir, it is quite peculiar."

The General answered, "It is.

Colonel Marsh asked, "A sign from Heaven?"

The General replied, "Perhaps." As the fire witches ears perked up, she slithered over to the officers and ran her sharp tentacles up and down the glass partition that held the ghost spirits captive.

She inquired, "Thinking of escaping are we?" She then bellowed out a hideous laugh with molten lava dripping out her mouth.

The General as hot steam began to scorch him, he screamed out, "You will be forever bound to this Hell. The Colonel and I, we will be free again."

The Union Lt. Colonel George Jameson heard what his General told the fire witch, as he was never too far from his commanding officer.

The marshland where they were held captive also contained monstrous mosquitoes, venomous snakes, spiders and all of other creepy things unholy to the human race. It reeked a foul putrid odor, of the other forms of life called demons. It was a dark and evil place for the Underworld to habitat. Yet on the other side of that ugliness was beauty of the dead that was almost astonishing. The Lt. Colonel slipped out of the cemetery unaware to the fire witch and reported to the Unknowns what he had heard.

He told them, "The snowfall seems to be a sign from Heaven that the General and Colonel's release is forthcoming."

A Union Unknown spoke, "How can we be certain Sir? Summer Ray hasn't been seen around these parts in years. Perhaps she lost faith in her General and us for that matter."

The Lt. Colonel Jameson assured the Unknowns, "Summer may have lost her faith in mankind, partially. I am convinced, however, she has not lost faith in her God. She will complete her mission."

Captain Xavier and other Warring Angels under his command, who are within close proximity of the cemetery, Praised God for His goodness. The Heavenly Host knew the Underworld would not go down without a fight. Captain Xavier would have to meet once again with Captain Talhelm in the outer regions to discuss battle plans, once the Spirit informed them the time. Summer Ray's instructions were clear. She needed her twin brother. Yet time was running against her. Little did she know, the General was slowly evaporating. Once fully extinguished, he would not be seen or heard from ever again, above the earth or below it. His disobedience to the Angel's orders to never leave Gettysburg, his time for redemption was running out. Like seeping sand through an hour glass, his time was short. The General saw the changes in his appearance through the reflection on the glass partition. If his cell mate noticed it, he did not mention it. Colonel Marsh's physique and stature did not change, as he died a Confederate hero. Summer knew nothing of the General McDaniels deteriorating condition. It was best she did not. Knowing the truth, would compel her to act hastily and put herself once again in harms reach. She needed Anthony and for now that was priority.

The Journey of a Million Miles

Christmas Eve at the Rockefeller Center, the ambiance of the Christmas lights and music, holiday shoppers, it is easy to get carried away with it all. Yet, to see the homeless by the droves, reaching out for buck to by a meal, Summer Ray stopped fast in her tracks. Her skates were hanging off her shoulder as her and her family passed by an elderly woman on the street begging. Her clothing was light and the shoes she wore had holes in them.

Summer exclaimed, "When I saw the condition of the southern soldiers at Camp Trousdale, there was nothing I could do to help them. I could not come back to our time period and bring them what they needed to stop their suffering."

As Summer asked her family if they would all pitch in to help this abandoned woman she continued, "However, we can all do something to help you ma-am." The family gave this freezing homeless woman close to $200.00. Other tourists who heard Summer's story reached into their pockets as well.

The Shaman ordered, "Anastasia, we must find our Anthony."

Summer looked at her and said, "I know." When Summer saw the look of urgency in her grandmother's eyes, she abruptly asked, 'Grandmother what is wrong? You look almost panicked. We will find him."

The Shaman answered, 'The question is not whether we will find him, but rather will we find him in time?" As snow was falling softly around them, Summer wouldn't budge until her grandmother told her what she knew. Summer demanded, "What do you know?"

The Gatekeeper replied, "Anastasia my dear, your General in Savannah is deteriorating. We are racing against time. If we do not get to him in time, he will be forever lost and tormented." A stunned Summer asked, "What are you saying? Will he go to Hell?"

Her grandmother answered, "I am afraid so. But he will be cast out to the greatest arm of Hell; the farthest and the most torturous place of all." Summer had to think. Then she inquired, "And the Colonel Marsh?"

The Shaman replied, "No dear. He died a Confederate Hero saving your life."

Kat asked, "How much time do we have?" The Gatekeeper sadly spoke, "Only but a few days!"

Summer exclaimed, "What? We have to find Anthony here and then go to Georgia like yesterday? This will be like trying to find a needle in a haystack. Oh my God!" The situation was damn near hopeless. At least with hope there are still possible solutions. Without hope, nothing is possible. Hope gives the ability to believe. Without belief, what is the point of trying? It simply is a waste of time.

Billy finally spoke, "We did not come this far to fail. Let's get to the Rockefeller and see what happens." With that, covered in snow, they made the final walk across the street to the ice rink. The Shaman and Gatekeeper ducked inside a nearby restaurant, while Kat, Billy and his mom waited in the rather long line to skate. Yes, it would close to a two hour wait. But the view was amazing. All the dazzling dancing Christmas lights, enhanced by Christmas music, as Kat kept a watchful eye out for any signs of Summer's twin. The temperature had dropped to a mere 30 degrees. Thankfully, the wind was quiet but storms were raging inside of Ms. Summer Ray Sherwood. Her thought that all this would actually work out okay, had eluded her. Her faith was fading and she was actually close to tears. Yet due to her pride, she refused to let them fall. She didn't want her son or best friend to know how close to breaking down she really was.

    This journey of a million miles seemed like it was all a mirage. She wondered if it were all but a dream and she would wake up once again in her own bed, dazed. No, such luck. This was all too real and all too right now. Time could not be frozen. Summer knew the General's free will of disobedience endangered his very existence. But, he refused to think of himself. He put her life before his own and that had too of meant for something. With all her heart, she believed that God was merciful. She knew He does not wish that any perish in Hell. So quietly she reminded Him of what the General did for her. How he too laid down his own life for the sake of her survival. Perhaps that would grant them more time or perhaps not. Only time once again would tell.

As the three finally made their way to the desk to pay for their skating, Kat once again stayed on the outside of the ice by the boards. She tried to stand exactly where she stood a few years before, hoping Tony would once again show up. Billy and his mom laced up their skates and headed out to the ice. Tony and Tyler his son both had the same kind of sacred bond with the ice as did Summer and Billy. Separated, but only by time and it was time to finally by re-united.

The Shaman and Gatekeeper were kept warm inside a nearby restaurant. With tall glass windows overlooking the ice, they could see sort of, what was going on. Christmas Eve, at 7:00 pm, will never grow old in New York City, a magical place. Though like Gettysburg, it had seen its share of death and destruction in the 19th Century as far into the 21st.

Acts of Terrorism

As Americans know all too well, on September 11, 2001, Islamic hijackers sent by Osama Bin Laden crashed four American planes into buildings, killing close to 3,000 innocent victims. Those killed were someone's father, mother, brother, sister, child, aunt, uncle, cousin, friend or sweetheart. The nations mourned at the catastrophic damage that was done to these great United States of American and to the innocent people who perished.

- American Airlines Flight 11, carrying 81 passengers and 11 crew members, at 8:46am at a speed of close to 467 mph, crashed into the north side of Tower One of the World Trade Center between floors 93 and 99.

- United Airlines Flight 175, carrying 56 passengers and 9 crew members, at 9:03am at a speed approximately 590 mph crashes into the south side, of the South Tower, of the World Trade Center between floors 77 and 85.

- American Airlines Flight 77, with 58 passengers and six crew members at 9:37am crashed into the western side of the Pentagon at a speed of 530mph.

- United Airlines Flight 93, with 37 passengers and seven crew members at 10:03 intended for Washington, D.C. crashed in an open field due to the brave passengers who rushed the cockpit, therefore resulting in a dramatic decrease in loss of innocent life.
Air speed at time of impact – 583 mph.

Shortly after the attacks, President Bush stated the following:

> "Freedom itself was attacked this morning by a faceless coward and freedom will be defended. The United States will hunt down and punish those responsible for these cowardly acts."

In a Press Conference addressing the attacks he also stated:

> "America and our friends and allies join with all those who want peace and security in the world and we stand together to win the war against terrorism.
>
> Tonight I ask for your prayers for all those who grieve, for the children whose worlds have been shattered, for all whose sense of safety and security has been threatened. And I pray they will be comforted by a power greater than any of us spoken through the ages in Psalm 23: "Even though I walk through the valley of the shadow of death, I fear no evil, for You are with me."
>
> This is a day when all Americans from every walk of life unite in our resolve for justice and peace. America has stood down

enemies before, and we will do so this time.

None of us will ever forget this day, yet we go forward to defend freedom and all that is good and just in our world.

Thank you. Good night and God bless America"

Although the Bush Administration did not see the victory of Osama Bin Laden's death, on May 02, 2011 close to the ten year anniversary of 9/11, the Obama Administration carefully targeted Bin Laden's hiding place and killed him. True to the words of the American leaders, the terrorist and many who stood beside him, were hunted down and destroyed. On September 10, 2013 President Obama spoke the following in regard to the Syrian government using Chemical Weapons:

"What happened to those people, to those children, is not only a violation of *international law, it's also a danger to our society.*

If we fail to act, the Assad regime will see no reason to stop using chemical weapons. As the ban against these weapons erodes, other tyrants will have no reason to think twice about acquiring poison gas and using them."

Because the Syrian government broke international law by using Chemical Weapons and slaughtered over 1,400 innocent men, women and children with poisoned gas, some Americans believed President Obama was right in enforcing a strike against those responsible, should the powers at be involving the United Nations, not settle the matter diplomatically. Backing down from terrorists, only gives them more room to do what they do best...terrorize! Yet once again, the nation is divided, as many Americans also oppose the strike.

Still, racism and rioting, bitter hatred, violence and murder, at times Summer wished the end of time would come sooner. But, that would mean and even greater number of the lost could not be saved. Was that the lesson of the Colonel Marsh's pocket watch? Is that why he gave it to Summer Ray in the first place? Ben Franklin once stated:

"Lost time can never be found again."

Yet what happens when time runs out…? What then?

The Sunken Road

Only two hours were allowed on ice per session and Summer Ray and her son's time had already passed the hour and half mark. Summer skated over to Kat and asked, "Any sign of him?"

A worried Kat answered, "I'm afraid not Summer." Summer waved to Billy and told Kat,

"Well I have to get out of these skates. I am starting to freeze. How are you holding up? Do you want some hot chocolate or coffee?"

Kat replied, "No! I will wait here a little longer." As Billy skated off the ice, he followed his mom to inside where the lockers were. He noticed the distraught look on his mom's face. He sat down next to her and hugged her. Next to her own salvation, Billy was her greatest gift from God.

Billy spoke, "Mom don't give up." Summer looked at her boy with a fake smile and said, "I am trying not to son. But maybe there are some things that I really cannot control. If we don't get to the General in time…"

When Kat also walked into the locker room, her best friend's face was sunken and sad. Much like the look on her face when Summer brought Kat to the Sunken Road at the Antietam Battlefield. It was Kat this time who flashed back to a few months prior. Summer was giving Kat another one of those unwelcomed history lessons.

The "First Battle of Bull Run" was fought on July 21, 1861, in Prince Williams, Virginia, near the city of Manassas. It was the first major land battle of the American Civil War.

Summer spoke to Kat, "Did you know that Yankee spectator's salivating for a Confederate defeat came out to watch the Battle of Bull Run?"

A dazzled Kat replied, "What?"

Summer answered, "Yeah! They set up camp with their carriages, ladies dressed in their pretty day dresses, kids even came to witness the bloodshed. The Yanks thought it would be a quick and easy battle that left almost 5,000 casualties and sent the Yanks running."

Kat inquired, "What happened to the asinine spectators?"

Summer replied, "Some were trampled by horses, blown up and some escaped. It was pretty much a give in to both the Union and the Confederacy, the war was going to be much bloodier, longer and costlier than the over egotistical Yanks thought."

Summer continued, "There was a poor elderly widow by the name of Judith Carter Henry who was bedridden. When the battle came near her house, a Union artillery shell crashed through her bedroom wall and tore off one of her feet. She died later that day from her multiple wounds. The horror of it all, just cannot and will never be explained or ever really understood."

Kat asked, "Summer, I don't know what voice told you to do what, but are you sure you want to open yourself up to more of this devastating blood, guts and war? When is it going to be enough for you?"

Summer somberly replied, "I wish I knew Kat. But, perhaps when their blood is justified and their sorrow is wiped off the blighted landscape on every battlefield. I felt it. I felt their undeniable suffering. It jumped into my soul and hasn't left.

Why I am burdened with it, I do not know. But, perhaps it is an honor to be able to feel them."

Kat shouted, "Honor my ass. You are always unhappy. Do you realize that? Other than seeing Billy and Emma and looking forward to holding Serenity Hope, you have lost your happiness and your zeal for life."

Summer took a deep breath and said, "I no longer know what happiness is. I don't even remember what it is."

Kat responded, "You live in your own beautiful home, have more pets than the Humane Society, even skating doesn't hold the same joy for you. What is it that has caused the ember of your passions to fade?"

Summer looked at her concerned friend and said, "Somehow I got caught up in a make believe world of the past and present. Dreams come true. I still have that conviction and I won't let it go. God has His reasons for all of this Kat. I just don't know what those reasons are. Perhaps once the land is no longer mourned, I won't have to either."

Kat replied, "Do you even know what you just said?"

Summer answered, "Of course not Kat. Do I ever know what I freakin say"

Kat demanded, "It's like you have taken the sanctuary of the dead soldiers on as your own personal tribute to them. What if you really cannot keep your promise to bring them peace? What then? Are you going to live the rest of your life in misery beating yourself up over a promise you made when you were barely a grown up yourself? No one would judge you Summer Ray."

Summer while driving put her head down for a split second and Kat instantly reacted, "That's it, isn't it? You are worried you will be blamed if you cannot make good on your word. Now it all makes sense. This crazy obsession with the General, the Unknowns and now this! You are afraid you will fail and failure to you worse than death itself. Oh my God Summer Ray let it go!"

As tears fell down across Summer's face, her reply was, "I can't. They need to go home Kat. Once we find Anthony, this battle won't seem so hard. Maybe then I can share the load, or won't feel so alone anymore. Ever since my accident, I have felt detached from the world. The ice was my only saving grace. But even that as you said, has lost its joy. I don't know what is wrong with me. The General is locked in chains and under that stupid witches spell. The Colonel J.D. Marsh who apparently saved my life, is and has been in that state for so long, I cannot turn my back on them. Whether it is for the Cause, for God or for my own stupid reputation, I do not know. But, I have to finish what I never meant to start. I knew I shouldn't have climbed that hill. But, call it fate or destiny, I can't turn back now. It is what it is and I know your here and will continue to support me."

Summer looked up at the Antietam Visitor Center and informed Kat, "Here we are!"

Kat, as she opened the passenger side door only stated, "Oh joy!"

It was again time to venture into a new passage of the unknown. What the ladies were searching for on this new voyage; rough seas, high waves, treacherous and dangerous turns, God would see them through. Summer Ray was going to finish her mission. Kat only hoped that conclusion came sooner than later. Her friend was aging before her eyes and Kat simply wanted her best friend "Ray Ray" back. Anthony had to be found. It was no longer a matter of if, it was now a matter of when, a determined Kathryn Black thought to herself. If Summer Ray wouldn't consult a medium to find out his whereabouts, she would talk to the Shaman herself. Perhaps there was something that could be done to expedite the process.

As Summer unpacked her camera and other assorted equipment from her camera bag, Katie texted the Shaman while Summer was distracted. If Summer knew of Katie's plan to find

Anthony, she would be furious. Summer's knowledge of the dark magic, quite possibly clouded her good judgment. Yet, Kat believed in the paranormal and if they could travel back in time, open portals with four leaf clovers, then there had to be a way to get to Anthony without offending Summer's religious beliefs.

The early morning text back from the Shaman startled Kat as it read, "I've been waiting for you to ask. The Gatekeeper and I will see you this evening in Gettysburg. Anastasia mustn't know."

Summer looking over her shoulder seeing Kati texting asked, "Is everything okay with the girls?"

Kat lied, "It's just my alarm. The girls aren't even up yet and we shouldn't be either. Come on... let's get this day over with!" As the ladies headed off to the Antietam Battlefield, Kat finally felt an end was in sight. Summer Ray needed to move on with her own life and as long as the General Michael Moses McDaniels was in chains, so was her best friend. It was time to move forward and release them both!

The Battle of Antietam

Sharpsburg, MD

The Battle of Antietam was fought on Wednesday, September 17, 1862 near Sharpsburg, Maryland and Antietam Creek. This battle was part of the Maryland Campaign. Many historians believe it was the turning point of the Civil War in favor of the Union, as up to that point, the Army of the Potomac had suffered devastating losses by the Confederates. The Battle of Antietam was the first major battle in the American Civil War fought on Union land. It is the bloodiest single day battle in American history, with close to 23, 000 casualties. Determined to get as close to the front lines of battle, Clara Barton did what she could, to help the suffering soldiers by bringing them food and water, and to help the wounded. Due to the bravery, compassion, and strength of heart, a monument is erected on the Antietam Battlefield in her honor.

Clarissa Harlowe Barton, though she went by the name of Clara, performed her first field hospital duties after the Battle of Cedar Mountain in Northern Virginia in August of 1862. The Surgeon attending to the wounded, immensely distraught at the devastation of human carnage and massacre encircling him, wrote of Clara Barton:

"I thought that night if heaven ever sent out an angel, she must be the one – her assistance was so timely."

Thus her name, "The Angel of the Battlefield" was given. At the Battle of Antietam, Clara while attending a wounded soldier stated:

> "A ball has passed between my body and the right arm that supported him, cutting through his chest from shoulder to shoulder. There was no more to be done for him, so I just let him rest. I have never mentioned that hole in my sleeve. I wonder if a soldier ever does mend a hole in his coat."

The brave soldier fighting for his Cause, found a new one as he lay wounded in Clara's arms. It is possible from her account, he saved the life of the woman who was desperately trying to save his.

Monocacy Battlefield

The Best Farm; Frederick, Maryland

Taking the war into Northern land, General Lee intended to divide his army into three sections in order to interrupt Northern supply lines, lower the Union confidence of winning the war and to capture the Union garrisons at Harpers Ferry and Martinsburg, West Virginia. On September 9, 1862 General Lee wrote out "Special Order 191."

Special Orders, No. 191
Hdqrs. Army of Northern Virginia
September 9, 1862

1. The citizens of Fredericktown being unwilling while overrun by members of this army, to open their stores, to give them confidence, and to secure to officers and men purchasing supplies for benefit of this command, all officers and men of this army are strictly prohibited from visiting Fredericktown except on business, in

which cases they will bear evidence of this in writing from division commanders. The provost-marshal in Fredericktown will see that his guard rigidly enforces this order.

2. Major Taylor will proceed to Leesburg, Virginia, and arrange for transportation of the sick and those unable to walk to Winchester, securing the transportation of the country for this purpose. The route between this and Culpepper Court-House east of the mountains being unsafe, will no longer be traveled. Those on the way to this army already across the river will move up promptly; all others will proceed to Winchester collectively and under command of officers, at which point, being the general depot of this army, its movements will be known and instructions given by commanding officer regulating further movements.

3. The army will resume its march tomorrow, taking the Hagerstown road. General Jackson's command will form the advance, and, after passing Middletown, with such portion as he may select, take the route toward Sharpsburg, cross the Potomac at the most convenient point, and by Friday morning take possession of the Baltimore and Ohio Railroad, capture such of them as may be at Martinsburg, and intercept such as may attempt to escape from Harpers Ferry.

4. General Longstreet's command will pursue the same road as far as Boonsborough, where it will halt, with reserve, supply, and baggage trains of the army.

5. General McLaws, with his own division and that of General R. H. Anderson, will follow General Longstreet. On reaching Middletown will take the route to Harpers Ferry, and by Friday morning possess himself of the Maryland Heights and

endeavor to capture the enemy at Harpers Ferry and vicinity.

6. General Walker, with his division, after accomplishing the object in which he is now engaged, will cross the Potomac at Cheek's Ford, ascend its right bank toLovettsville, take possession of Loudoun Heights, if practicable, by Friday morning, Key's Ford on his left, and the road between the end of the mountain and the Potomac on his right. He will, as far as practicable, cooperate with General McLaws and Jackson, and intercept retreat of the enemy.

7. General D. H. Hill's division will form the rear guard of the army, pursuing the road taken by the main body. The reserve artillery, ordnance, and supply trains, &c., will precede General Hill.

8. General Stuart will detach a squadron of cavalry to accompany the commands of Generals Longstreet, Jackson, and McLaws, and, with the main body of the cavalry, will cover the route of the army, bringing up all stragglers that may have been left behind.

9. The commands of Generals Jackson, McLaws, and Walker, after accomplishing the objects for which they have been detached, will join the main body of the army at Boonsborough or Hagerstown.

10. Each regiment on the march will habitually carry its axes in the regimental ordnance—wagons, for use of the men at their encampments, to procure wood &c.

By command of General R.E. Lee

R.H. Chilton, Assistant Adjutant General

Copies were given to each of his commanders. However, one of the copies was lost at the Best Farm in Frederick, Maryland. On September 13, 1862 a soldier from the Indiana Regiment found a copy of the order wrapped inside an envelope with a few cigars. The order was given to Major General George McClellan, commander of the Army of the Potomac. Upon being given the copy McClellan stated:

"Here is a paper with which, if I cannot whip Bobby Lee, I will be willing to go home."

Sadly, on September 17, 1862 at The Battle of Antietam, only four days after finding the "Lost Orders," 23,000 men became casualties. It was never clear if McClellan use the information gained from "Special Orders 191" to fully engage in destroying Lee's Army. Some historians believe he certainly had the knowledge to do so, but failed in his mission. On November 7, 1862 McClellan was replaced by Major General Ambrose

Burnside, in which the Burnside Bridge at the Antietam Battlefield is named after.

CHAPTER FOURTEEN

The Hard Rock Cafe

Christmas Eve always held a sense of longing in Tony's soul. For some odd reason he never quite felt whole, like there was something or someone missing and he just could never quite put his finger on it. He had great parents, an amazing talented son, his job, his skating, and of course his beloved New York City. Life should have been fulfilling for him. He was spending this Christmas Eve in Times Square at the Hard Rock Café with a few of his firefighter buddies.

Time Square at any time of the year is bursting with night life; the drinking, the dancing, the lights, the people and even the noise of the traffic with their honking horns, the sound of the roaring fire engines as they passed by always exhilarated and gave Tony an adrenaline rush. He didn't need drugs or too much alcohol to have a good time. He had his city. He was as close to New

York City as Summer Ray was to her beloved Gettysburg. Two cities located on the East Coast of the United States, both drenched with history. Yet they are as different as night and day.

Tony was still a bachelor. Other firemen who he considered brothers, took him out for a few drinks. Timmy was there from the Bronx department Rescue 3. Doug stopped by from Brooklyn 9, as well as a few of the guys from his own department Ladder 219.

The Hard Rock Café in New York City started with Eric Clapton's guitar hanging on the wall. Then Pete Townshend's of 'The Who' also provided one of his guitars. This grew into over 70,000 guitars of other artists hanging on the walls or on display at this famous café. It's a great atmosphere, amazing food, as well as pretty cool memorabilia from other stars such as Billy Joel who donated his 1974 Moto Guzzi 850 Eldorado motorcycle; The Beatles colorless suits; and The Romanes black leather motorcycle jacket autographed by the band, to name a few of the items on display.

The crowd had gathered on Christmas Eve much like every other night in the café. People from around the world come and visit it, as they do the small historical town of Gettysburg. As the guys were drinking a few beers and having a hell of a "New York Minute," Tony, for some strange reason, felt the need to turn to the left of where they were sitting to the entrance of the café. His heart almost stopped as he saw two familiar ladies walk in. As Summer Ray glanced over in the direction of the bar, as her eyes lifted to that of her twin brother. Their two souls collided and it almost took her breath away. Kat finally caught on and also looked over at him. Her breath was almost taken away as well, but for a totally different reason.

Timmy sitting next to Tony noticed who he was looking at and said, "What is with you man? Go talk to them and ask them to come here for some drinks."

Tony said, "I met the one on the right before, last year at the Rockefeller Center." He thought for a moment then said, "It was a year ago Christmas Eve and the other one was on the ice."

Timmy thought the coincidence was rather odd as he quizzically asked, "Christmas Eve?"

Before Tony could catch his own breath, Kat and Summer Ray walked up to the bar. Seeing how there was no time for small talk, Summer Ray looked directly at her twin brother half sitting on a bar stool, one leg on the floor the other on the bar stool, with a Margarita in his hand and demanded to know, "Are you Tony Trousdale?"

Stunned that the ladies knew his name, he replied, "Are you stalking me? Not that I mind it and all. But how do you know my name?"

Kat introduced herself as the woman who stepped on his boot at the Rockefeller Center a year before. Summer bravely said, "I am Summer

Ray. I know this is going to sound crazy, but I believe I am your twin sister."

The drink Timmy had just taken, upon hearing what Tony's sister just said, he spit it out in shock.

Tony chuckled and answered, "Sorry about my bad mannered friend here. But I don't have a twin sister."

Kat spoke, "You were born in Savannah, Georgia were you not?" Tony flashbacked to the dream that had haunted him, about being a Major in the Confederate Army, as Kat said the exact same thing that woman did in his dream.

Summer asked, "Does the name Bryce Alexander Benjamin have any meaning to you?"

Tony's face went as white as the napkins on the bar. No one but him knew about Bryce Benjamin. He used to have nightmares about being in the Civil War and one dream in particular troubled him. He was the Confederate Major Bryce Alexander Benjamin. He knew he had almost slit the throat of some woman claiming she was his twin sister.

Tony leaned into his friend and asked, "What the hell did you put in my drink man?" He then turned to the ladies standing before him. "If this is real," he thought, "she will have the scar."

Tony stood tall to his feet, almost afraid of the answer but bravely asked his twin sister, "Do you happen to have a scar on your neck?"

Summer Ray now close to instant tears replied, "Yes!" Then her feistiness came out when she added, "And with no thanks to you. You damn near killed me!"

When Summer Ray moved the collar of her shirt out of the way, for him to see the scar, Tony damn near fell to the floor. The shock of what was taking place weakened his knees as he answered, "Oh my God! It's true." He then practically fell on his twin and as the two siblings locked in an embrace, Tony's eyes fell across Kat's face. When the truth hit him like a ton of bricks, he side stepped toward her and while still hugging his twin he spoke, "It's you. You sat with me on the rocks in Tennessee."

Kat so in love with him only whispered, "Yes!"

Tony began to introduce the ladies to his friends at the bar, but before he could order their drinks, Kat stepped in and said, "Tony, we must take you with us. Please it urgent. We will fill you in on the way."

Summer stated, "Our grandmother is around the corner waiting to meet you. But you and I must get to Savannah."

Tony seeing the look in his twin's eyes said, "For one, you are not leaving here without me and we have a grandmother and she's here?"

Kat stated, "Time is running out Tony. We must leave and leave now!"

Tony didn't waste another second. He said his "goodbyes" to his friends and left the café with the girls. Once outside the café Times Square, as usual, was lit up like Christmas, only in this case, it really was. Tony looked at his watch and saw that it read, "12:12am." Before wishing his twin and Kat a "Merry Christmas" he looked up toward heaven and said, "Christ is indeed the reason for *this* season!" They then walked in the direction of the Shaman and Gatekeeper in a nearby restaurant. When the Shaman suddenly saw a falling star outside the restaurant window, she knew the answer was forthcoming. She grabbed her husband's hand and said, "He's found!" The elderly couple thanked God for his goodness, kissed each other and headed outside in the light snowfall to the sound of Christmas music, people laughing and frolicking in the snow, and the best part of all was when her grand-daughter Anastasia spoke words she was longing to hear for the past fifty two years, "Grandmother, I would like you to meet your grandson, Anthony Trousdale!"

CHAPTER FIFTEEN

Newly Reunited

It was only a few days after Christmas and only a few days before New Year's Eve, December 28th. The newly reunited family was celebrating inside by the warmth of the fireplace in Gettysburg at Summer's house. Kat took an urgent phone call and went outside. Tony, on the drive to Gettysburg, called his son Tyler to let him know the amazing news. Tyler agreed to drive to his Aunt's house in February after his present tour was finished with. The questions remained, "What would happen once the General and the Colonel JD Marsh were freed?" "Would Tony and Tyler move to Gettysburg, or would they stay living in Manhattan?" Summer Ray wasn't about to let her twin get away again and already started discussing the possibility of them moving in with her for the time being.

Thirty Years Prior

Outside on the deck, Kat was smoking a menthol cigarette trying to listen to whoever it was on the other end of the phone line. The snow had encased the trees as if nothing or no one could turn the world upside down. The beauty of the white snow blanketing the ground covered whatever dirt was underneath it. Kat engrossed either with the phone call or at her winter wonderland, suddenly remembered the scripture, *"Though your sins are as scarlet, they shall be as white as snow."*

She started to reminisce about how she had to rescue her best friend from off the ice and snow covered Big Round Top close to thirty years prior, while her friend was in shock from so much blood loss when she felt and ripped open her hand on a thorn bush. Kat, then found herself recollecting how immensely terrified she was when she got the call from Summer Ray's father about her horrific car accident. When Katie (back then) asked her best friend's dad if Summer would survive, through his tears he could only answer, "We don't know."

For Kat, the possible death of her beloved best friend at such an early age almost caused her at times to overlook her own happiness. Summer's face with a broken nose and cheek bones, was swollen and bruised from hitting the dashboard. She wore her seatbelt but the force of the impact was just too much. Back then, in the early 80's, air bags were not a requirement. When it was evident that Summer suffered brain damage, Katie vowed to never leave her best friend no matter what while she sat by Summer's bedside before she regained consciousness.

Yet in her heart Kat knew, if she could go back and relive the past thirty years, and make changes to her own life and go off in a different direction without Summer Ray, Kat knew she never would. Kat was right where she belonged all along and was ecstatic that Tony was finally found. Kat caught herself daydreaming about marrying him. He lit up her life and she was silently hoping she lit up his as well.

Her Sacrifice

Meanwhile, back inside the house, Summer and her twin were discussing flight plans to Savannah, Georgia and how they needed to leave the following morning. Knowing the General McDaniels was almost lost to them, they decided to fly instead of drive. Although Summer hated flying, it was just one of those things she had to do. Her twin would be with her and that gave her a great sense of comfort. The nightmare of the fire witch would soon be over. The Shaman couldn't have been happier to see her two beloved grand children finally by her side. The ability to still live a dream echoed loud and clear. Life was renewing itself and Summer, for the first time in what seem to be a life time, her heart was soaring. Yet, that elation and her high spirits were both about to be brutally cut short.

When Kat came back in the house to join the others, Summer looked at her best friend's withdrawn face and instantly knew something was terribly wrong. She ran over to Kat by the sliding glass door and asked, "What is it?" All eyes were on Kat and in a broken voice that only Summer Ray could hear, Kat softly spoke, "I have breast cancer. The doctor said it was both breasts and they need to do an emergency mastectomy."

A shell shocked Summer Ray Sherwood, could hardly believe her ears. The only response she could muster up was, "What?" Wasn't she just about to leave for Georgia to help free those men? Kat began to cry and informed Summer, "They said I need to be in the hospital by 6am tomorrow morning to prep me."

"Summer Ray," Kat wailed as she grabbed onto her best friend, "You have to go to Georgia. You must keep your promise." Summer through her tears started screaming at whoever was able to hear her, "No! I won't leave you Kat."

A concerned Tony stepped in and asked, "What is it?" When Kat informed the truth to the rest of Summer Ray's family, the silence exploded so loud that everyone heard it. This could not have been happening, not now at such a critical time in history.

Kat spoke, "I had the tests done before we left for New York. At my routine mammogram they found something and sent me for more tests. I just got those test results a few minutes ago. But if they don't operate, the cancer could spread to the point it will be inoperable."

Summer adamantly told her best friend, "I am going with you in the morning."

Kat demanded, "He will be forever lost Summer Ray. You will never see him again, is that what you want?"

Summer exclaimed, "I won't leave you in your own hour of need Kat. I can't. You stood by me through everything I have ever gone through. I woke up in Shock Trauma and your face was the first I saw."

Kat said, "Love doesn't keep score Summer Ray. You are not in debt to me."

The Shaman spoke up, "Anastasia, you must go to Georgia as planned. Kathryn will have the rest of our family and hers to stay with her."

Summer Ray before she stormed outside angrily informed them, "No! I won't go and leave her like this."

Summer ran toward her favorite boulder as her insides were ripped to shreds. She could barely breathe as the reality of the circumstances fell upon her. In one split second, the universe once again had seemed to have tumbled over her and she was left beside herself with grief. How could she leave her best friend of over forty years and go and rescue spirits who were not even alive? She was being tortured from the inside out and upside down, while her best friend was now fighting for her life. There was no choice. Summer knew she would not leave her best friend to fight alone. The decision was set in the boulder she rested her head upon. She would not leave in the morning for Georgia.

As her twin brother approached her, just the sight of him, gave Summer a sense of peace. She knew the two of them would never again be separated as he was the closest blood relative she had. They shared the womb together and would have to learn to reunite. The devil may have stolen their birth mother and their first fifty years together, but they'll make damn sure he won't steal the next fifty!

Tony spoke, "Summer Ray, whatever you decide, I will stand with you."

Summer grabbed her twin brother's hand, "I can't leave her Tony. I will have to live with the demise of the General for the rest of my life. I just don't know how I am going to be able to do that. But for now, Kat needs me and I have to be strong for her."

When Summer and Tony came back inside the house, everyone knew the decision was made and Summer was not to be talked out of it. She turned to Kat and said, "I won't leave you!" With that, the rest of the day and night went on in great sadness. Kat mentally took it all in and said nothing about her best friend's decision as they began to make arrangements to make Kat as comfortable as possible and to plan for her treatment after she left the hospital. Kat's family was on their way to Gettysburg to see her. In time of great need, troubled waters and broken bridges, one can only do the best one can.

The next morning, Kat was admitted to the Frederick Memorial Hospital, where Billy, Ella, Ellodie and Emma were all born at. A few weeks prior, Summer Ray was the happiest she had ever been in a very long time, as she held her precious grand-daughter in her arms. This morning, she was like a Zombie walking the halls of the hospital beside her best friend. Summer Ray as promised did not leave Kat's side. She held her hand as they wheeled her close to the operating room. Kat had tubes and machines hooked up to her and Summer silently cried and prayed for her best friend to pull through the operation. Suddenly, Kat yelled to the hospital technician to stop. Summer and everyone else stopped short as well.

Kat spoke, "This is as far as you go Summer Ray."

Summer confused asked, "What are you talking about Kat?"

Kat responded, "I will not have you break your promise on account of me."

Summer began to cry, "No! It isn't on account of you Kat."

Kat grabbed Summer Ray by the arm and shouted, "Listen to me. In the event I don't survive the operation, will you deny my last request?"

Summer began to get hysterical, "You will survive Kat. Don't talk like that!"

Kat inquired, "Yes! But in the event I don't, would you deny me my last request?"

Summer Ray whispered, "Of course not Kat?"

Kat turned to Tony, "I request you take Summer Ray out of here and you leave for Georgia immediately!"

Summer screamed, "No! You can't do that to me Kat. Kat, No! That isn't fair...You can't do that to me."

Kat barely awake could only say, "I am not doing this to you. I am doing this for you." Her sacrifice, ripped through the heart of everyone standing there.

Tony, Billy and the Shaman tried to console Summer Ray. But as they wheeled Kat into the operating room, as the door slammed shut behind them, Summer was despondent. She collapsed on the floor as she could hardly believe what her best friend had just said.

Billy was at his momma's side and said, "Mom! You have to go to Georgia. We will be right here when she wakes up. You cannot deny Aunt Katie."

Tony and Billy then helped Summer Ray to her feet. She looked back in the direction of the operating room and whispered, "I love you Kat." She said nothing else to no one and walked without any feeling whatsoever in the direction of the "Exit" sign. A numb Summer Ray Sherwood would be on the next flight out of Baltimore to take her and her twin brother to Georgia. Come hell or high water, Summer knew she had to honor the sacrificial request of her best friend! Come what may, whether she saw Kat alive again or not...

The Journey Home...

OTHER BOOKS BY AUTHOR

Summer Ray – Series

This Fair and Blighted Land

Volume 1

Savannah's Calling

Volume 2

The Journey Home

Volume 4

The Blessings of Liberty

Volume 1

The 150th Anniversary of The Battle of Gettysburg

Special Photography Edition

With Jason Shindledecker

NOTE FROM THE AUTHOR

    I am woman who ultimately fears God and who absolutely believes there is a Hell waiting for anyone who does not believe, in nor accepts, the Lord Jesus Christ as their own personal Lord and Savior. I have never been one to cram God down anyone's throat, nor am I one to preach, "hail, fire and brimstone." I believe in doing so, does more harm than good. I am by no means a religious woman. I am simply a woman who loves God and believes in Heaven and in Hell. I have never been one to beg for anything in my life. But, I am so convinced there is a Hell that I am begging you, if you are not yet saved to read a book titled: "*A Divine Revelation of Hell.*" It is authored by Mary K. Baxter. You can find it at most bookstores or online! This is probably the scariest book I have ever read. I wish I could buy it for every human being alive on the planet today! But, since I cannot, I can only refer it.

Although I am an author and a publisher, I am a Christian first. It is my prayer, by writing this series, that the truth of good vs. evil, will ultimately be portrayed in such a way that it will become real to you – the reader, and you, too, will make the decision to make Jesus Christ the Lord of your life! I added the following in case you are ready to make such a decision:

> "*For God so loved the world that He gave His only begotten Son, that whoever believes on Him should not perish but have everlasting life.*" John 3:16

"If you confess with your mouth the Lord Jesus Christ and believe in your heart that God raised Him from the dead, you will be saved. For with the heart one believes unto righteousness, and with the mouth confession is made unto salvation. Whoever calls on the name of the Lord shall be saved." Romans 10:9 – 10-13.

Father, in the name of Jesus Christ I come to You. I am a sinner Lord and have sinned against You and against Heaven. I ask you Lord Jesus to forgive my sin and to come into my heart and save my soul. I ask that I be born again into the family of the Living God, and so escape the fires and the torments of eternity in Hell.

I give my life to You. I ask that You will help me to serve You from this moment on. I thank You for saving me and for redeeming me by Your precious Blood. Amen!

My book titled: *"The Blessings of Liberty & 25 Devotions on Freedom, Liberty & Justice...God's Way,"* will also assist you in your walk with the Lord. The following is an excerpt from the back cover.

- Biblically sound – promoting the truth of God's Word
- Historically sound – Revolutionary & Civil Wars, Civil Rights Movement
- Gives insight to the darkest hours of the wars and how our Forefathers persevered through their belief in God
- How our choices today affect our lives tomorrow
- How some of our founding documents are used out of context, therefore promoting demoralization, debauchery and death
- Showing the REAL love of God to those who are ensnared by the devil
- Promotes a positive self image in knowing who you are in Christ

- Gives understanding and insight to the demonic influence surrounding oppression, depression and possession

Round Top Publishers & Productions
Contact and order information – front of the book

Made in the USA
Charleston, SC
07 September 2014